PRAISE FOR ÁINE GREANEY

Áine Greaney has her finger on the pulse of the transnational Irish experience and the challenges of contemporary feminism. Trespassers brilliantly engages themes of aging, gender, sexuality, and the family to depict an empowered but entrapped Irish diaspora in the throes of identity formation. Simultaneously rife with nostalgia for home and the fierce desire for success in Cape Cod and greater Boston, Greaney's collection is an exemplary illustration of the Irish immigrant presence in New England.

— ELLEN SCHEIBLE, PROFESSOR OF ENGLISH AT BRIDGEWATER STATE UNIVERSITY AND AUTHOR OF *BODY POLITICS IN CONTEMPORARY IRISH WOMEN'S FICTION: THE LITERARY LEGACY OF MOTHER IRELAND.*

What a perfect title Áine Greaney has put on this poised and closely wrought collection. Her characters (most of them Irish women) dwell in spaces where they never feel completely at home. One woman feels that there is "a constant scrim between herself and the world;"another reveals that "dark things flit around the edges of her mind, like a wasp at the window." They are indeed trespassers into awkward emotional terrains—and their successes are usually triumphs of adaptation and endurance.

— JAMES SILAS ROGERS, AUTHOR OF *IRISH-AMERICAN AUTOBIOGRAPHY: DIVIDED HEARTS*

Praise for Áine Greaney

Áine Greaney's new collection of short stories, *Trespassers,* is an admirable addition to her elegant, engaging body of fiction spanning more than two decades. A County Mayo native now living in Massachusetts, Greaney's characters reveal what it means to be an Irish woman making her way in the world today, whether it be in New England or Ireland. Greaney's voice is authentic and her ear for dialogue and cadence is unerring. Greaney's characters weather impulsive love affairs, unexpected pregnancies, disappointing marriages and the long journey home to bury a parent, but they shoulder their burdens with grace and humor, even as their flaws and foibles get revealed. Despite their travails, Greaney's characters remain sturdy and optimistic, as if the promised land is still waiting to be discovered. This is a collection of stories to savor.

— Michael Quinlin, author of *Irish Boston*

PRAISE FOR ÁINE GREANEY

Who hasn't once lamented "I don't belong here!" The characters in Trespassers join that cry from a compelling variety of situations. Thanks to Áine Greaney once again for writing so powerfully from the land off the other, we hear them loud and clear, whether the voice (and you will so clearly hear voice!) is that of a child new to the land of divorce, a mother chafing at life in an in-law apartment, a single wedding guest who offers lodging to a stranger, a teen on a work visa who might end up with a very living souvenir of a one-night stand. Webs of connection to Ireland and America cling to each story, but don't overshadow the universality. I know I won't be the only one who raced through these stories like morsels from a box of sweets, realizing I had only so many to enjoy while I kept on reading.

— SUZANNE STREMPEK SHEA, AUTHOR OF
BECOMING FINOLA

TRESPASSERS

AND OTHER STORIES

ÁINE GREANEY

Sea Crow Press

Contents

"There is an internal landscape, a geography of the soul; we search
for its outlines all our lives."
— *Josephine Hart, Irish-born author*

"The ache for home lives in all of us, the safe place where we can
go as we are and not be questioned."
—*Maya Angelou*

TRESPASSERS

AND OTHER STORIES

TRESPASSERS

ANTHONY SULLIVAN LIMPS down the pebbled driveway where their Subaru car is parked, its back seat still stacked with boxes. It's their annual move-in day to the Cape Cod summer house, and this year, it's hard to say which creaks more—their old front porch and steps or his new replacement knee.

"Where are you off to?" Elizabeth, his wife, calls from the weathered, shingled house with its green-painted windows.

"There are things to do here."

He turns. Since this morning's drive down here from Boston, Elizabeth has pinned up her long, gray hair.

He points downward: "I need to stretch this thing out."

No answer. Instead, as she turns to latch the front door open, that gray top-knot waggles like a disapproving forefinger.

After 53 summers down here, he still mixes up the names of all her ancestors' portraits that hang along the house's hallways and upstairs landing. Though not Josiah, whose name is carved into the house foundation. In 1887, Josiah Charles Lunt bought and cleared this land to build this estate over an inlet of Nantucket Sound.

Oh, well. At least the afternoon sun is coming out, and the knee pain is easing, and he's already at their white, wooden sign propped in the front lawn: "Private property. No Trespassing."

Before the roadside pillars, he crosses a wedge of lawn to the shortcut to the wooded trail that's strewn with acorns and winter-brown pine needles. In the woods, he swats at something buzzing near his neck, then stoops to stuff his trousers into his socks. Ticks. She has a horror of them.

"Fools," she often says. "Only fools take stupid chances." The trousers tucked in, he straightens up, teeters, then walks on.

The rest of the year, on his winter walks across Boston Common to his volunteer job at Legal Services, he almost forgets this place, the way you forget how a highway rest area once looked or felt. Then, every year, their Boston cleaning girl helps them drag the seasonal storage boxes and suitcases from their city brownstone to the Subaru.

More than the woodland ticks, Elizabeth Lunt Sullivan fears beach trespassers.

The summer tourists could never find this summer estate at the end of a dirt road. But every year, a few locals sneak through these woods to the Lunt estate's private beach. Year after year, he assures her that these visitors are harmless and he asks why they should deny the native year-rounders a swim in the ocean or the chance to watch their kids building sand castles?

Three summers ago, on a hot August day, she dispatched him down the avenue because she'd spotted a car parked in the grass, right next to their "No Trespassing" sign. When she arrived, the local police woman looked hot and bored inside her uniform shirt. Elizabeth interrupted the young officer's rote questions to say, "Listen, it's all fine and dandy until one of these types trips or falls on the rocks down there. Then, it'll be lawyers and compensation!"

That day, Anthony longed to interrupt, to remind his wife that *he's* actually the lawyer in this house. He also wanted to cite the Massachusetts statute that permits public usage of the inter-8 tidal area for fishing, fowling and navigation. Plus (he's always wanted to add) this statute was legislated by the 1640s British colonists, who, of course, were this territory's first trespassers.

Before this blasted knee business, the best part of move-in day is this walk and his annual treasure hunt for whatever the locals have lost or left behind on their beach. Used condoms.

Empty wine bottles. Someone's washed-up shoe. Last year, he found a woman's blouse stretched across a rock. He'd stuffed it into his old chino trousers and sneaked that blouse up to the house to hide it under his mattress.

For years, their daughter Louise and her husband, Mark, and their twin boys used to drive up here from Manhattan. For two weeks of the summer, the house and gardens and the beach were suddenly loud and busy. And, when the kids got bored, they drove up the dirt road to enter that *other* Cape—the loud, frenetic world of miniature golf and clam shacks and restaurant patios packed with half-naked tourists.

Now, Jonathan and Eddie, their grandsons, are in graduate school, and, for the past five years, Louise has made excuses for why they can't come north anymore.

This far into the woods, the trail is strewn with a few fallen branches. Wait! There's a tire track here, too. It's actually *two* tire tracks, each snaking around and over the other, and these tire tracks are far too wide for an ordinary bicycle. He follows the tracks between the trees to wood's end, where two scarlet-red bikes stand propped against a scrub oak.

Anthony pulls up his shirt sleeve to measure these bike tires against his own forearm. Yes, these tires are extra wide, but there's nothing dangling from the red frames or clipped to the bicycles' carriers. So today, who has pedaled down here?

He crosses to the clearing for a straight-on view of the inlet.

Out there, the lobster buoys always remind him of scatter pins in a woman's hair. Except for the seagulls squawking from the old fishing dock, there's nobody down on their beach.

OK. Let's try to get down the stone beach stairs, at least half way. One step. Anthony wobbles, then steadies himself. Damn it! Right. On the second step now, so let's try for the third. His legs won't obey. Not today. Just wait for the pain to ease before starting back up.

He built these stone beach stairs. It was 1966, when he and Elizabeth had just started courting. *Courting.* Now, that word jigs around inside his head, like some old children's ballad: *A frog went a-courting.*

That hot July 4th weekend, her two sisters and the sisters' boyfriends—the young set—had sailed out of Boston Harbor. The three girls were in cotton blouses and pedal pushers and short-sleeved dresses. The boyfriends wore linen shirts over tennis shorts. After their Saturday morning tennis, two of the boys carried the beach blankets and wicker picnic baskets, while the girls stepped from rock to rock, arms spread and screeching at each other not to fall.

Anthony Sullivan, the son of a stone mason, suggested that they all collect the longer, flatter rocks to braid and pound them into the sandy cliff.

Yeah, he had the wrong surname and the wrong Boston accent. But his widowed mother had scrimped and saved and pushed him toward a scholarship to Sacred Heart College. From there, he went to Suffolk Law, where a professor had gotten him a clerkship at Lunt, Wigglesworth & Lodge.

Two months after he started at that downtown firm, he met the boss's daughter and wife. As he shook hands and smiled, young Anthony felt like he was meeting duplicate versions of the same woman.

Over the years, in some mean part of his consciousness, he's often wondered if he'd courted and proposed to Elizabeth Lunt as an act of youthful disruption.

The night they built these beach steps, he shared one of the two 10 guest cottages with a guy called Peter, her sister Jane's boyfriend.

While Peter snored, Anthony listened to the sea washing up between the rocks. He dozed and, each time he woke, he was convinced he'd heard Elizabeth's steps outside the cottage's screen door. But even back then, young Elizabeth Lunt lived by the rules.

Right. The knee is a tad better now, and there's still no sign of anyone down here. He'll just totter back to the house and help her with the rest of those moving boxes.

He's up the steps and back on the trail when he hears voices.

Turning, he spots a young man and a woman walking along the tide's edge. Naked.

Up there at the house, if she's airing out the upstairs, she'll spot this couple, and there'll be another mortifying police call.

Down there on the beach, the young girl stops and bends over to scoop something out of the wet sand.

Keep going. But Anthony stays, staring down and across the beach at the girl's globous breasts.

He's almost back at the scrub oak and those bicycles when he hears the footsteps crunching behind him. It's that young man, and he must have cut up across the beach rocks. Still naked. Can you be in violation of the public nudity laws if you're on private land?

This fellow heads Anthony off on the path. "So did'ya see enough down there, asshole?"

"I'm just out for a walk, actually." Anthony keeps his gaze fixed on a little scar that sits below this man's clavicle. "Now, if you'll excuse me here." He motions to detour around him, but the naked fellow blocks him again.

"Listen, Bro. I don't appreciate you getting off on watching my girlfriend and imposing on us here." He grabs his own crotch. "So if I were you, I'd fuck off back to your nursing home." He angles a fist toward Anthony's chin. "Like, before I do something I could get arrested for here."

Anthony stops again, convinced he's heard those bicycle spokes tick-ticking, those fat tires squelching through the spring mud behind him. He turns. Nobody back there.

At the house, the Subaru doors are slung open now, and Elizabeth has left one of the moving boxes perched on the wicker rocking chair on the porch. He stoops to lift it.

Inside, she's dragging the old dust-cover sheet off the couch.

The gray top knot has loosened.

An upstairs door slams shut. His knee throbs. He stumbles with the snap-lid box. Turning, she looks vexed. Then, a crease forms between her eyebrows, as if she's noticed something new about her husband—something *hunted*.

He sets the moving box atop the mahogany bureau that's stuffed with three generations' worth of musty board games.

She asks, "Well? Find anything or anybody down there today?"

In his mind's eye, he sees that naked girl stooping over the beach sand, her bottom pitched toward the sky.

"Um ...What?" He asks, buying time, hunting for the best lie, the exact words.

She shouts: "I *said*, 'did you find any–'"

"No," he interrupts. "Well, I had to clear a few fallen branches. Probably from that storm back in March. But nothing else."

A Fine Lady Guest

ON THAT LAST evening of my sun holiday, I asked that island boy for what, all along, I'd actually wanted. I suppose you'd say they were ordinary requests, really, and certainly not what you'd think a 58-eight-year-old woman like me should have to pay a 20-year-old island boy to do.

So that night when I went to his cabin with the hens clucking outside the door, I knelt on his bed–the same bed where, for nine previous nights, we had done all those *other* things.

I asked him to kneel behind me and to massage my scalp. Then, as his hands rubbed my head, I told that boy, that male prostitute, all my troubles. I blathered on about getting passed over for the vice principal-ship at my school, where I work. And how my younger married sister, Margaret, never helps out with our widowed mother who, back home in Ireland, has come to live with me. In fact, Margaret had even made a fuss about me taking this sun holiday.

Oh, yes, he had to listen to a tale of woe, for sure, but that boy massaged and "uh-huh'd" quite well. Plus he said that so long as he got paid his usual, it was all the same to him.

Afterward I withheld his cash payment to demand that he walk me back up the beach to the Bougainvillea Resort, where I was staying.

I can still picture us back there, strolling along that white sand, hand in hand like a real couple. Once we reached the cluster of resort lights I said, "You know, real gentlemen walk a lady all the way to her door." It came out crankier than I'd intended, and I heard how funny and, under the circumstances, how *absurd* that "gentleman" bit sounded. But he didn't seem vexed at all, and anyway, back home or abroad in these hot, holiday places, I believe in reminding these kinds of people who's the paying customer.

"Local boys are never allowed on resort property." He enunciated these words like he was making a grand, megaphone announcement. Or echoing something he'd been told and told, or that *he'd* told or repeated to scores of pale or sunburned women like me.

"Sure, I won't tell a soul," I said, suddenly bolting across the beach, my dress fluttering as I prayed to hear his breaths and his steps behind me. Sure enough, he caught up and took my hand again.

We stood at the bottom of the Bourgainvilla Resort's rear stairwell, well out of sight from the hotel reception. I handed him his cash, including a 20-euro tip. Then, for the first time in that entire fortnight, he fingered my face. This touch, this tenderness made me want to hold on and weep.

"Goodbye, fine Irish lady." He whispered it into my hair before ducking under the eaves to stride away into the island dark.

Later, in the dead of night, I woke to a thwap-thwap sound out there, somewhere underneath my room. I pushed back the cotton quilt, rushed to slide open the French doors, thrilled that 14 he'd changed his mind and now, he was down there pitching pebbles toward my balcony.

In that humid night, all I could see were the lights across the bay. All I could hear was the sea in its slow, lazy creep. So no.

No island boy. But as I lay back into my bed, I swore I could feel his hand in my hair, massaging my scalp.

Next morning, I woke up later than usual. Downstairs, the street outside was barricaded, and a constable in his khaki uniform stood diverting all traffic around the Bourgainvilla Resort.

"What happened?" I asked young Sophie, my favorite waitress, who always gave an extra boil to my tea water and always let me use my own (Barry's Irish) tea bags. In answer to my question, little Sophie said that, after my departure today, she would miss me very much. That I was her favorite lady guest.

Oh, yes. One hundred percent.

I pulled a cotton sun hat from my handbag and took my cup of tea outside to the pool patio. The German and British and American guests were already guzzling their bottles of beer.

But this morning, I sensed something new, something frizzling around those umbrella tables.

"What?" I asked Antoine the barman. "Please tell me what happened."

"A most regrettable occurrence, Madame, but our Bourgainvilla lady guests are always safe with us. And now, allow me to make for you my goodbye guava cocktail?"

I reminded Antoine (again) that I didn't take booze at this hour, and certainly not with my morning tea.

The street had opened up and the constables were gone when my airport taxi man parked and got out to open the car boot for my suitcases. Actually, it was the same fellow who had delivered me there, though he didn't seem to recognize me.

As we drove off through that town, the hot wind through the rear car windows turned my thighs sticky damp. Over the racket from the car radio, my driver inquired if I had fallen in love with their beautiful island. Or—and here, he flashed me a cheeky look in the rear-view mirror—if I'd fallen *in love* on their beautiful island.

I shook my head, *No*.

"Our town hall, Madame," he nodded toward a lemon-hued building, the centerpiece of the cobbled town square. When he raised his arm to point it out, I spotted a folded-over newspaper on his passenger seat. The above-the-fold headline: POLICE SHOOT RESORT INTRUDER.

"My cousin's boy," the driver said, following my gaze toward that newspaper, that black-and-white photo of that boy whose hand I could still feel in mine.

"Our island police and these big, rich men who buy up our hotels." He rubbed his thumb and forefinger together to signify money and payoffs. "All last night, all morning, my cousin, my aunt, my mother, we all weep, weep, weep. Only 20 years of age, and always such a very good boy."

Hmm... not as good or saintly as you think, I thought, as I pictured that boy above me in his tatty single bed.

In that high, brittle tone that I use with the fidgety or extra slow learners in my school classroom, I interrupted the taxi driver to inquire what year their town hall had actually been built.

"1823, Madame."

"Fancy that," I said.

Of course, thanks to the brochures back in my room—the room that was now being hoovered and scrubbed for some new guests, I already knew all the answers. But there's nothing more awkward, more *funereal* than a silent taxi journey.

A mile on, we passed a school with a playground full of running children in brown shorts and bright yellow shirts.

"Tell me, at what age do they all learn English?" I asked.

In the rear view, he frowned, puzzled, like I'd asked a very stupid question.

"Yes," he said. "We must all learn the Queen's English."

After the town I inquired about the pickup trucks parked just off the road, while a dozen men and women stooped and labored in those scorched-brown fields.

At the airport he left the engine running as he walked around to fetch my suitcases from the boot. I paid him his fare, and I watched his eyes widen at the 50 Euro tip I pressed into his fist.

"To help with the funeral," I said.

My taxi man gave a courtly little bow, and, just like Sophie the waitress, he said I was a fine lady guest.

Twelve Weeks

IT'S SATURDAY NIGHT AND, instead of being down at the pub as usual, here I am patrolling these pharmacy shop aisles, checking each overhead sign: Allergies. Analgesics. Cough and Cold. Hair care.

I've just cycled up here, so, even in this over-air-conned pharmacy, I'm sweating like a bloody pig.

Family Planning. OK, this is me, and, honestly, I could laugh out loud. I mean, what *eegit* of a marketing person thought that

"Family Planning" was a good name for these shelves full of condoms and pregnancy tests? More like family *UN*-planning, right? 'Cos like, a fortnight ago, when I left that beach party with that American guy (Joshua? Jason?), I definitely wasn't planning anything—well, except; well. You know.

Clear Blue. First Response. Plus: The shop has its own brand of preggers test which is a bit cheaper.

I drop the Clear Blue box into my shopping basket, then look around for where they keep the cold drinks, which I'll need for tomorrow morning.

"Pedal 'n puke." That's what I've started to call my morning cycles from the workers' hostel over to my summer job at the Canoe Beach Hotel and Resort here on Cape Cod where, if you haven't copped it already, I'm over here from Ireland as a J-1 summer student.

And so far, being a J-1 student means scrubbing toilets and hoovering out hotel guest rooms full of beach sand and pizza boxes and, sometimes, a baby's dirty nappy on the floor.

"Diapers," Deneisha, our supervisor, informed me nappies are called over here. That morning, I was so hung over from the night-before 'sesh,' that I had to bite my tongue not to just blurt it out: "Listen, where I come from, shite is just shite."

The pharmacy checkout woman in her red shirt looks nearly as old as my granny back in Cluainard, County Galway.

"Find everything you need, Hon?"

I drop a packet of tissues into the basket, too, 'cos the hay fever over here is just mental.

"Grand, yeah," I say as she squints at my work T-shirt with my name stitched above the hotel logo on the pocket. "Sarah," it says, though my name is really Sorcha, which, of course, is Irish for Sarah. But look, I'm over here to earn some dosh, not give language lessons, right? So for this summer, I'm Sarah.

"Rewards card with us?"

"What? Um ... No."

Beep! Goes my bottle of Gatorade. *Beep!* Goes my Clear Blue preggers test and my tissues. Then, I hand her my cash and get back some coins which, by now, I can actually recognize and name: Quarters. Dimes. Nickels.

"Have a good night," the woman says, as if I weren't standing there unzipping my backpack to drop in a test that'll tell me whether, at 19 years of age, the reason my boobs feel so bloody sore is because I'm preggers. Or maybe I'm not.

Earlier tonight, before cycling up to that pharmacy, the usual gang of us were all down at The Kilkenny Bar & Grill, AKA, "The K." With all its Riverdance-y music and that beer garden that's really just a few tables and sun umbrellas plonked onto the backyard tarmac, "The K" is the kind of place we wouldn't be caught dead in back home. But Séamus, the manager, who actually lives over here in America--like, with a house and a wife and everything--never hassles us about our fake IDs. Plus, "the K" is great 'cos it's easy for a lot of us to walk or cycle to from work.

Tonight, as I sat there amid all the beer and the jiggy music from the bar's outdoor speakers, that awful word— *pregnant*— kept thudding against my forehead. My third Coors Light only made it thud louder. So I told Joanne, who's one of my roommates down at the workers' hostel, that I had to go to the loo.

That wasn't a lie, 'cos these days, I always do—like, have to pee.

After the loo, I slung my backpack into my bike basket and pedaled up to this pharmacy.

As well as the day-and-night heat over here, Cape Cod is just one traffic roundabout after another, and I'm sure I look a right *eegit* now, waiting to wheel my bike across to the next median and then the next.

OK. No traffic now, so here I go, and shouldn't someone be playing some sort of cartoon-y music as I push on these rusty handlebars and trot across?

By the way, I got this bike at a yard sale for only twenty bucks, and the fella selling it looked so dodgy that, now, I keep expecting someone in one of these cars to roll down their car window and shout, "Hey! That's my stolen bike!"

Six months ago, when I was nearly half-way through my first college term down in Limerick and when I found that GO-USA website and applied for my J-1 summer worker's visa, it wasn't only for the money and the beaches.

Like, do you know how morto it is when your parents split up? Especially in a small village like Cluainard where, one day, your Dad just packs up his stuff to move a half-mile down the road to his brother's rental holiday home? Trust me: It's really cringe stuff. And look, don't get me wrong here. I know it's worse for Mam, and I've a thousand questions to ask her about it all.

But now that I'm over here and away from all the unspoken words and all the *drama*, I do feel a lot more chill.

You know what will make me even more chill? When this preggers test in my backpack shows negative. Yeah. Like, that'll stop me concocting daft stories about that night at that beach party.

Joshua/Jason *had* actually worn a condom. Right? *Yes. Deffo.* I was bollocksed drunk, but I remember that pause or break in the action. And I remember that part that the guys never want you to watch, when you're supposed to just lie, silent, as you listen to the condom packet getting torn open. Right? Yeah? So all these queasy mornings and the nighttime throb in my boobs are just from being away from home. Or it's the stress of Dad doing a runner.

Twenty minutes after leaving the pharmacy, I turn off the road and wheel the bike up the steep avenue toward the hostel's back door.

This old hostel place has dirty windows and nobody cuts the grass, but the back gardens have a lovely sea view.

The first few days here, I took a walk around and found some old park benches and a few stone statues sitting in the middle of some weedy flower beds. Someone here said this used to be a religious retreat place. But now, the American *padres* or nuns or whoever have sold this three-story building to the Canoe Beach and Resort.

Did I mention that the place has absolutely no air-con—which, just like the total lack of public buses over here, is something the folks at Go-USA "forgot" to tell us?

I hoist my bike up the hostel's back steps and, inside, park it next to all the other bikes propped against the community-room wall.

My bedroom is on the third floor. But I'll use the downstairs loo, which sits at the end of a creaky corridor, and where I'm much less likely to bump into someone I recognize.

Someone in Room Number 6 is snoring. In Number 9, I can

hear a girl yap-yapping on the phone in a language that I don't recognize.

The shared loo with its two big hand basins is even hotter than the corridor, but it's only for three minutes. That's what the back of the Clear Blue box says. It even has a sort of alarm.

And 99% accuracy. Right. Here I go: Unzip the backpack, open the box and hold that white thing under my pee stream. Then, I have to set it up on the cistern to wait.

Earlier, when I'd just arrived at the pub, my phone dinged. It was Mam. So I didn't bother opening that text. Until now.

"U OK? Saw on the news about another shooting over there. A shopping center? Please text back when you get this, Mam. XXX."

In our weekly Monday video calls, I've tried telling my mother that Cape Cod *isn't actually* America, and really *not* dangerous—like, unless you count those mental drivers at the traffic roundabouts. Actually, it feels like Canoe Beach and this hostel and "the K" are a billion miles from how I imagine the real America.

Well, I can't text her back now, not when it's nearly four o'clock on a Sunday morning over there and she and my younger brother Pádraig, or Paudie, are still fast asleep and I'm sitting here on a toilet waiting for a preggers test to ding.

Mam would make a lovely granny. *No. Stop. Stop thinking that.* But the more I try to stop thinking about it, the more I picture my mother and me, walking down the village wheeling a baby buggy. In that snapshot, I've left college and left Limerick and I'm back there in Cluainard forever and ever.

Shite. Someone just opened the bathroom door. Who? I bend over to gawk under the door. Tanned legs. Pink flip flops. One of the Romanian girls? Swish. Swish. She's brushing her teeth. *Christ, hurry up, before this thing dings.* A spit. Water running. Then the pink flip-flops heading back toward the door, which slaps shut.

Ding!

It's as clear as the nose on your face. That's one of my Dad's old-fashioned, country expressions. Maybe the Clear Blue people should put that on their advertising. Because now, as I stare at this positive test, Dad's voice is right here in this American toilet: *Clear as the nose on your face.*

The positive preggers test in my shorts pocket presses against my thigh as I creak up the hostel stairs. Phone dings again. It's Joanne, the one who, earlier, I'd sneaked away from at"The K."

"Where U? We going down beach. See u there?"

"Going z-z-z-," I text back as I picture the whole gang walking down the beach road, phones glowing in the dark and the off-license bags of booze rustling.

Magda, my other roommate, is fast asleep. Maybe because she's Polish and not part of our Irish gang, I have this daft moment when I wonder if I should wake her up to tell her the news: *Guess what? I think I'm pregnant.*

On our first night here, the three of us girls sat on our single beds, each of us trying to be dead cool as we exchanged names and universities and what each of us is studying back home.

Magda waved a hand between me and Joanne. "You know each *other*? Like, in your country?"

Earlier, I'd spotted and heard Joanne on the airport bus from Boston down to Hyannis. It was actually hard *not* to hear her, as she kept on boasting to her seat-mate, a fella from Sligo, how she was in pre-law at Trinity College in Dublin.

When Magda asked if we knew each other, I said it really fast: "Oh, Jayzus no!" Magda is a pre-med student in Krakow.

When it was my turn, I tried to upsell or make my teacher-training or education college down in Limerick sound better than it is or will ever be.

Over a year ago, when I was studying for my Leaving Cert and just after Dad left, the art teacher at my community school helped me to get my portfolio together, and she and the career guidance counselor gave me a list of fantastic-sounding art colleges.

At home, Mam turned really fussy. What do they call that?

Like, a helicopter parent? She kept going on about how a woman needs her own salary and a secure pension and couldn't I be drawing and coloring on my own time, as a little hobby for myself?

Then she said how, back in her school days, if she hadn't been sensible and gone for that job in the bank, where would we all be now?

I wanted to keep life easy and not add anything that'd make my mother look more stressed than she already looked. So here I am, a year into teacher college now, where it feels like some avatar of myself is sitting in lectures or trekking across that quad, while the thought of a classroom full of kids absolutely terrifies me.

Most nights, it's just Magda and me here–while Joanne is still out doing whatever—or, rather, doing *who* ever. Mornings, when the seagulls start going mental below on the beach, I hear Joanne creaky-tiptoeing up the stairs and across toward her bed.

Now, Magda doesn't move or grunt as I undress in the dark and ease myself into bed where I try not to whack my head against the slanted ceiling. I shove that preggers test under my pillow because I can't throw it in any of the hostel bins. *What they don't know won't trouble them.* That's another one of Dad's old sayings.

I pull my knees up and wrap my arms around myself. I listen to the usual hostel noises —a door banging, a toilet flushing, music from the next room.

Lying here, I imagine I'm back in my old childhood bedroom. The house smells of breakfast porridge. Dad's backing the tractor out the yard gates. Mam, dressed for work in her green bank uniform, is standing over my bed to get me up for school.

I work Sundays at the resort, so next morning, I turn off the road and cycle across the small, empty car park for West Canoe Beach, which is smaller and rockier than Canoe Beach. I shove the bike's front wheel into a bike stand and cross to the portable loo where, inside, I heave up half of a McDonald's burger and all of last night's Coors. Once I'm finished, I throw the preggers test in there, too, where it floats on top of all that shit and vomit and wads of loo paper.

I don't have to clock in at the resort until half past seven. So I grab my backpack and Gatorade from the bike basket to go and sit on the sea wall.

Gargle, gargle. Glug. Glug. Nobody wants a hotel house-keeper with vomit breath, right? And if I lose my job, I lose my J-1 American visa and I'll have to go back home where I'll have to concoct a reason *and* find a doctor–like, one who can keep their gob shut. *What they don't know won't trouble them.*

I walked up this little beach that night with Joshua (I've decided to call him that). He had to help me up the stone beach steps over there. Where was his place from here? He said that cottage was his folks' place, but he was crashing there while working some kind of summer internship for some kind of aquatic-y science stuff. His room smelled of damp clothes, and the cottage had two front doors—one an ordinary door and a second one with a net in it—like, for midges or mosquitos or whatever.

This morning, the seagulls are swarming and squawking over something dead washed up on the beach. Down there to the left, I spot a thin rope strung between a few spindly wooden posts. Oh, yeah. I remember now.

That night, Joshua stopped there to show me what he called a nesting area for these little birds that are endangered and need to be left alone to breed. I remember drunk-laughing at that.

Didn't I crack some joke about bonking birds?

Now, I hop down off the sea wall and walk down the beach to read the printed sign: "Canoe Beach is a great place to raise a family! All Cape Cod beaches are designated nesting areas for piping plovers, and it is against the law to ...." *Blah, blah, blah.*

A great place to raise a family. Was this someone's idea of a ha-ha joke?

As I pedal the half mile over to the resort, I remember my Mam telling these stories about the old days, like, when Ireland had no legal abortion and girls had to travel to England–to 'take the boat.' She said it happened to a few of her friends, but now, over here, I remember that funny voice she always had when she talked about it.

Wait! Had she actually been one of those girls herself? I picture her sitting alone on a big ferry and, afterward, in a London clinic where she had to give a fake address and help the nurse to pronounce Bríd, which is her Christian name. Isn't there a name for a story like that? Like, where you're meant to learn something? Oh, yeah. A parable, like the seven fishes or whatever.

The Canoe Beach Resort WiFi is way, way better than the hostel, so in Room 15, I switch on the hoover and leave it running right inside the door where Deneisha, my boss, will hear it from the corridor. I sit on one of the room's two double beds where, honestly, I'd love to just flop backward and go back to sleep right here, on top of this duvet with its pattern of blue starfish. I type into my phone: "Abortion, Ireland."

There's a lot of stuff about the 2018 abortion referendum, which happened during my last year at school, AKA, the year Dad left. The electricity poles in town were plastered with signs and pictures of unborn babies. On Saturdays, Mam kept the kitchen radio blaring as people called in and got into fights about the whole thing. Honestly? I remember wishing it would all go away, but I also remember how delighted Mam was when the country voted in favor.

Yes, just like I thought, the Irish Health Services website says that a 'termination' in Ireland is free.

Brilliant! Wait! Here's something else: 12 weeks.

"You can have an abortion if your pregnancy is no more than 12 weeks, which means 84 days since the first day of your last period. After 12 weeks, you can only have an abortion in exceptional circumstances."

"For fuck's sake!" I say it out loud, hoping the hoover noise drowns out my voice.

Here's more: "There must be at least three days between being certified by a doctor and having the abortion procedure .... This delay of at least three days can give you time to decide ... There may be delays in getting an appointment with your GP or doctor ... This could delay an abortion ...."

I've never been good at Maths, but as I finally start to hoover the carpet in Room Number 15, I calculate that if I'd shagged Joshua just last night, this 12-week rule might— *might*—work.

But my flight ticket back to Shannon Airport is for the 26th of August, so these delays mean that I'd land over there and not be able to do anything, except, like Mam's "friends,' maybe sneak over to England.

I'm back on my phone, checking the flights from Shannon Airport to Gatwick, when someone clanks on the hotel-room door handle. It's Denisha, with that clipboard of hers. "Sarah?

How soon can you get finished in here? Room 16's a real doozie."

I haven't a clue what 'a doozie' is, but it doesn't sound great, right?

On Monday, my day off, I drag my arse out of bed to cycle (four roundabouts—but who's counting?) to this urgent care medical place that do official preggers tests. On the way back, I stop at the library that actually looks like someone's house, not a place with free books and computers and two good printers.

This time I type in: "Cape Cod, Abortion." Up comes a place called Health Corners, a 'women's health' place up in Boston.

Come on! There's nothing down here, on Cape Cod?

Health Corners offers an at-home option. Oh. My. *God*.

That's just perrfect. You have to have your own bathroom and a few days off from work and, afterward, a place to do a

"mandatory" computer "telehealth" visit with "a clinician."

In the library, a gray-haired woman who smells of perfume smiles across at me from her computer station. Next to her, a man with mean, slitty eyes is on some website with the noise so loud it's coming through his headphones. Another man is heavy-breathing at his computer monitor. Nope. I can't talk to a doctor or nurse in here, not even with earbuds in. But if you actually go up there—like, to Boston—the website says you can drive yourself home after "your procedure."

"Eight hundred and fifty dollars!" Are they actually serious? I make $15 an hour here, minus what they take out for my hostel room. Shit. So no more beer sessions up at "The K" for me.

"You look awful tired, Pet," Mam says later, on our Monday afternoon video chat.

I'd just cycled home from that library in time to drag one of the hostel's benches across the lawn to outside the community room window for their shitty WiFi. I always perch on the of the bench, so that behind me, Mam can see the marsh and the sea and the sail boats against the sky.

On the grass sits my backpack, where I've stuffed all the printed information about that Health Quarters place up in Boston.

Behind Mam's right shoulder are the two clothes-drying racks that she's set up inside the glass kitchen doors speckled with rain. She tilts her phone toward my brother Pádraig on the couch, who's gawking down at *his* phone. "Look! Doesn't our Sorcha look shocking tired?"

Over the back of the couch, he gives me a lazy thumbs up.

"Anybody dead?" I ask in a teasing voice, because when I ring from college, I always get the list of who's died in the parish and if there was a big crowd at the funeral.

"Nobody dead," she says, with a cheeky grin. "Not this week anyways. Though did you hear the McManuses had their baby?"

"No, I didn't hear that," I say. "That actually *wasn't* in the local paper over here." My hand auto-drifts to my tummy which, of course, is still flat—even flatter now that I spend my mornings puking and my days scrubbing hotel rooms and my afternoons asleep.

Mam notices. "Have you a sick stomach? I bet it's that

American junk food. Take a few spoons of bread soda in a drop of warm water."

"Em ... Yeah. I saw a box of bread soda inside in the hostel fridge."

"We're really looking forward to you coming home. I already booked the day off from work to go down and collect you at Shannon."

"Yeah, me, too," I say. Then I wonder: When those airport doors slide open, will my mother notice, like, magically read something new in my face?

Years ago, when Paudie and I were kids, we secretly called Mam the "*sionnach*," or fox. And trust me, there's a reason why we nicknamed her that.

She says, "We'll have a barbecue. Like, if the weather is anyways fine at all."

"Will you invite Dad?" It's out of my gob before I can stop it.

She frowns. "Ah ... no. Actually, I haven't seen a light below in the house."

"Did he move? Like, get his own flat?" *No. Please say no.*

Because his own place—not his brother's holiday home—would make things permanent.

Mam's voice turns high, false-cheery: "Maybe he's off on a sun holiday. A woman at the bank was saying she got a brilliant deal to Portugal—an apartment, the flight and the whole works!

But for the barbecue I'll invite the usual neighbors and the McManuses and the new baby and that new family who moved down from Dublin. And yourself and Paudie should invite your school and college friends!"

"That'd be brilliant," I say, even though, except for some chat while waiting outside a lecture hall, I haven't actually made any friends at college.

"So what other news have y–".

"–Em ... I actually have to go here, Mam. I ...err .. myself and the gang always meet for an evening swim down the beach."

For our last two calls, I've clicked off early and fast, just in case "the *sionnach*" sniffs or notices anything.

"Please be careful over there, Pet, and enjoy the rest of your holiday." We blow our usual kisses and, behind Mam's back, Paudie gives me another thumbs up.

Guess what? Mam's bread-soda stuff did the trick, so I no longer need that morning vomit stop on my way to work. And did you know that, in America, you can pee in any restaurant—even the posh ones? Yeah, you just get on your phone and have this whispery "conversation" while marching right in there and avoiding eye contact with the restaurant hostess. Oh, and did you know that the dollar stores over here have all sorts of really cheap stuff, like these cans of black and white beans and these ramen noodles you can just heat up in a guest's hotel room or, if it's dinnertime, in the hostel kitchen? Plus, in the dollar store across the road from "The K," I found a lovely sketch pad and a giant packet of pastel pens for only a few dollars.

I haven't told any of the gang here my news. After my afternoon naps now, instead of cycling up to "The K," I bring a can of cider out to the hostel's scrubby lawn where I sit on a blanket doodling or painting in my sketch book.

It's lonely being preggers. It's a quiet loneliness, not like when Dad left. Or, long before that, when Mam and Dad had a wedding or something to go to, and they used to leave us to stay our granny's house.

The preggers lonely is like you've hit the button and stepped right off the carnival ride of friends and party and beach. Now, I stay in my own, silent bubble and it's actually kind of cool.

"I'm not supposed to," I tell Séamus, the manager up at 'The K.'

"The J-1 student visa only lets you work for your sponsoring employee, which is the Canoe Beach Resort."

It's my Monday morning off; the pub's not open yet, and I have to shout over the radio blaring from the pub kitchen.

Séamus says, "Listen, if the arse-scratchers down in

Washington want to send their own kids up here to scrub restaurant dishes or bus tables, I'm all for it. Put them on a bloody bus and we'll put those little feckers to work! Or maybe the politicians should come back from their summer break to pass some legislation so we can hire more workers—like, people who actually *want* to do the job."

Séamus hires me to work three nights a week as a dishwasher —under the table and a cash gig. Yahoo! With my resort money, this'll be enough to pay Health Corners *and* arrive home to Cluainard and Mam with some cash to show.

By the way, I've been back to that little public library to research and send some emails to my top-choice art college, which is in Leicester, England. They have a portal where you can upload your application portfolio. So now I'm waiting with fingers crossed. If they like my stuff, I'll get invited over there for a campus visit. Can you believe it? Amazing what you can do and who you can talk to when your head isn't muzzy from a load of Coors and vodka shots.

If I get accepted at Leicester, how will I break this news to Mam? Or Dad? Honestly? I haven't a bloody clue.

I've been dishwashing at 'The K' for two weeks already, and it's really not that bad. Tonight, the 11th of August, has been extra busy, and the two chefs are already sitting out at the bar with their freebie drinks. So it's just me in this roasting hot kitchen.

I'm absolutely shattered tired as I cross to the dry goods shelves to steal a few packets of black pepper. I need the pepper for early tomorrow, to call in a sneezing sickie with Deneisha at the resort. I slip the pepper packets into my pocket and lift the two black rubbish bags out of their bins to head out to the dumpster.

Outside, beyond the high, slatted fence, it sounds like everyone in the K's beer garden is even more bollocksed than usual.

Is it? Shite. No. Yeah, it's that guy, Joshua the American! He's walking, car keys jingling, toward the rear car park.

"Sophia?"

I keep heading toward the dumpster. "Sophia?" He says it louder.

"Actually, it's Sarah."

He cartoon-slaps his forehead and takes me in, head to toe, including my white dishwasher's apron. "Yeah, yeah. Sarah. Um... how *are* you?"

I set one black rubbish bag on the ground. "Ah ... not so bad, yeah. And yourself?"

"I thought you worked at a hotel here?"

Thanks to you, and your shitty cheap condom, I work here, too.

"Yeah, you know. I like to stay busy. And you ... em ...Joshua. Have you finished your college internship studying those birds or fish—the ones that're endangered?"

"Ah, it's Jason. Yeah, my internship's done now, and the folks and my sister are up at the cottage from Connecticut—so I'm just hanging."

For one, daft minute, I imagine just blurting out the news to him, right there next to The K's old dumpster: *Hey, bucko, you're kind of a Daddy now.* I imagine him blinking at the news and me.

Shock? A smile? Or some mad invitation to go back to that cottage where I can meet his "hanging" family so we can all make some kind of transatlantic "parenting plan."

"Lovely." I say. "That sounds like great fun."

He points toward the rubbish bags. "Well, looks like you're busy and I gotta get going. So ... ah .. yeah, listen, have an awesome trip back home to Ireland. And it was really nice to meet you!"

Next morning, once I call in a pepper-sneezy sickie to the resort, I have to uber it up to Hyannis where I take the bus up to Boston for "my procedure." Yeah, that's what the woman at Health Corners called it on the phone.

The bus lets us all out at Boston's South Station where

everyone is rushing along the footpaths as if the day and the city aren't jungle hot—like, so hot that you can actually see the heat trapped under the overpass and glinting off the cars. By the time I walk to the city transit, or T station, the sweat is trickling down between my boobs.

I take two trains, and the second one takes forever and ever.

But at last, here's the station announcement and name that the people at Health Corners had told me to listen and watch for.

I wait to cross at the traffic light. Hah! Just like the Cape Cod roundabouts, but no need for the cartoon music here. As I wait, I picture one of the pastel paintings I've been working on out back at the hostel. Remember those old statues I found in the garden? I've actually sketched one, but with huge, spindly trees growing wild out of its saintly head, the branches reaching all the way into a fiery red sky.

There's a load of people standing around over there, just outside Health Corners. Had someone tripped and fallen? They all look like old-age pensioners. No, there are a few kids and their mothers, too. Hold on! Why are they gawking over here, watching and waiting for me to cross?

The traffic light changes. Walk sign comes on. These people don't look like a crowd of muggers, but still, I check the cash rolled up and shoved down into my shorts pocket. A young lad, only about 12, holds up a placard: "Pray to end abortion."

Jesus bloody Christ! Now, an old man with a big belly inside a green shirt blocks my path toward the clinic doors. Christ, I'm totally going to lose the plot here and get right in this fella's puss to remind him that, even in his young days, he could never *get* pregnant. And that maybe *he* should spend his summer cleaning "diapers" out of filthy hotel rooms and scraping half-eaten burgers and fried clams into kitchen rubbish bins.

The man hisses into my face: "Don't! Don't put a mortal sin on your soul!"

The Health Corners doors open and two women in matching pink bibs with a big logo on the front, are at my side.

One of these pink-bib women ushers that old fella back toward the street. "Buffer zone," I hear her say, as the other one puts an arm around my shoulders. "You're OK, Honey. We're volunteers and we're here to protect you."

I shake myself free of her. She grabs my elbow. "If you're having second thoughts, you should still check in for your appointment. We have counselors who can—"

I interrupt her: "—No second thoughts."

Then, I tug myself free and march, alone, toward those glass doors.

HOUSE DEVIL

AUDREY DESADORA WAS DRIVING over to Cedarville and the beauty salon for her Wednesday wash and blow out when she came upon a road construction crew. A local cop stood diverting everyone down Route 112 where, just a quarter mile on, Audrey spotted a roadside sign: "Your Summer Theater Needs you! Volunteer Today!"

The sign's hand-painted arrow pointed down an unpaved dirt road lined with dry stone walls. She couldn't be late for her weekly hair appointment. Most important: The day after tomorrow, Friday, when her husband Alfonsus arrives down here from Boston to the Cape, he'll do his usual odometer check on her car. *Screw it.* She'll just call and cancel the hair appointment and do her own bloody hair. When he checks through her credit card statement, she'll say that the stylist actually canceled on her.

She'd outfoxed him like this before. Like last summer when she'd gone to see that divorce lawyer in Hyannis. Back then, the lie and mileage subterfuge had worked. The lawyer visits didn't.

At the end of the pot-holed road stood a huge, brown barn with a wood shingle exterior that had seen better days.

"Woods Hollow Theater," said the sign over the wide door.

Inside, under the high windows, stood a line of fold-up metal chairs stacked against the wall. Against the rear wall was a cut-out room with a cheap, plywood door and another sign: "Theater Office."

"Hello?" Audrey called outside that office door as something skittered in the rafters above her head.

This was a stupid idea anyway. Even if she did get herself a weekday volunteer theater gig, Alfonsus would get wind of it, and then, there'd be real hell to pay.

Pity. Because, except for Jimmy, their aged landscaper, and Tracy, the hair stylist she'd just blown off, these Cape summers are long and lonely. There have even been some Friday nights when she was actually glad to see Alphonsus' Porsche Cayenne turning in their driveway.

A street angel and a house devil.

Back home in County Leitrim, her mother, long dead now, used to say that about those parish men who were all full of church piety and guff while their wives and kids wore thread-bare clothes and looked perpetually terrified.

Street Angel. House Devil. In this empty barn, Mam's old phrase beats a rhythm inside Audrey's head, like those skipping-rope songs from their village school playground: *Street angel.*

House devil.

Outside, a door banged shut. Footsteps crunched across the barn's front yard. Audrey turned to see a young woman in the barn doorway, blocking the afternoon light. Long blond hair. A huge, baggy sweater. A smell of French fries from the white paper bag in the girl's hand.

"Can I ... help you?" The girl asked. "We're not actually open for the season yet." About 25, Audrey calculated. Maybe 28.

"I'm here about your sign. About the summer volunteering? I'm Audrey."

The girl frowned, as if a 45-year-old woman in an Ann Taylor blouse and ironed Versace jeans was not what that roadside sign was supposed to attract. The girl swished back her thick, curly hair and remembered to smile.

"Sure! Oh, great. Yeah. If you want to just follow me? By the way, I'm Romney."

Looping around the metal hooks on the office back wall, Audrey spotted a long skipping rope–except that it was wire and, beneath it, on one of those fold-out chairs, sat what looked like the seat of a child's swing set.

Romney said, "All our performances are out back, and, as an outdoor, seasonal theater, we need heavy marketing—social media, our e-newsletter, ads, get on a few of the local podcasts and arts programs. Any marketing experience, Anna?"

"Audrey," Audrey corrected. "My name is Audrey."

Whatever was in that white food bag smelled so, so good, but of course, it was way, way off Audrey's Keto diet. "No," she said. "No marketing experience."

In fact, except for being Alphonsus Desadora's wife and the Irish-accented, schmoozer-in-chief for his Boston-based property-development company, Audrey had no professional experience at all.

Romney flashed another smile. "Oooh- *kay!* Yeah, no probs. Well, look, em ... Audrey. Why don't I take your name and contact info and then, once we're closer to opening night, I'll be in touch? Maybe we could train you to be one of our fillin or on-call ushers?"

Audrey gave the land-line number for the Cape Cod house, but with one digit off, so she'd never hear from this Romney kid again.

"What *is* that?" She asked, nodding at that looping skip rope behind Romney's head.

"Rigging," Romney said, through a mouthful of French fries. "A few summers back, we got it for one of the kiddie pantomimes, but we're all done with children's programming. Too many CORI checks for the volunteers, and all those hurt and cursing parents when their kids didn't snag the lead part. And the trash guys won't take it."

Romney set down the fast-food bag to stretch her arms wide,

like Jesus on the cross. "It's actually just airplane cable. You stretch it between two toggle bolts, one at each end of the outdoor stage. Then, one hard kick-off and Peter Pan goes flying!"

One hard kick. Flying. An idea flickered inside Audrey's head.

She said, "My husband owns a real estate development company. He contracts for those giant commercial dumpsters—you know, for when they're gutting a remodel. I could get rid of it for you. I could take it away now!"

"Really? Wow! That'd be awesome!"

Shit. The car clock showed 2:30. She still had to get that odometer reading up there to corroborate her hair-appointment trip.

Audrey reversed and turned the car and started back up that dirt road. The pebbles pinged against her car doors and that black garbage bag full of that Peter Pan rigging jiggled around in the car trunk.

At Route 112, the public road, she imagined reversing back down to the barn again. Up, down, up and down, as the odometer numbers ticked upward and while, inside that barn, Romney set down her French fries to post on social media about the crazy lady with a weird accent driving laps outside.

No, she'd just drive on toward Hyannis and stop at that mangey little strip mall where she can spend some of her secret cash stash on a bottle of cheap hair dye. Alfonsus doesn't tolerate graying roots. Or an un-botoxed upper lip. Or any public signals that his younger wife is turning less young.

Next day, Thursday, Audrey watched from the front living room window for Jimmy the landscaper.

"The Mister." That's what Jimmy always calls Alfonsus. The Mister was on the phone there yesterday, and he definitely wants that shrubbery along the fence trimmed.

Sometimes, after a particularly fractious weekend with Alfonsus, Jimmy's soft voice and his gifts of morning take-out coffee, bring a teary lump to her throat and makes her wonder:

Did this old Cape Codder with his weatherbeaten face smell the proverbial rat or, in her mother's words, the house devil?

Ah. Here, at last, was Jimmy's white pickup turning into their circular driveway and heading around the back of the house where Audrey would meet him at the back door.

Jimmy frowned up at that theater rigging looped over the door of the garden shed.

"Where exactly does The Mister want this?" He sounded suspicious.

"Stretched between that tall oak out back, and our bedroom balcony." She dropped her voice to a whisper; flashed him a flirty smile. "Oh, and it's me that wants this, Jimbo, not 'the Mister.' So not a word."

She winked at him. "It's our anniversary soon and this is my little surprise for him!" As he reached for that theater rigging, she knew he was picturing something really quirky.

Twenty-five years ago, she'd met Alfonsus up in Brighton, where she'd tended bar at that Irish-American pub. Back then, he called himself Al.

Thursdays, when the local construction crews crowded into the front bar, Al Desadora, a short man with tiny eyes, swished in to buy his crew—most of them Irish like her—a round of Miller Lights and Budweisers. He always left her a 10% cash tip, and then bustled off while his guys slugged their free beers and muttered curse words toward his retreating back: *Wanker!*

Bollocks! Wouldn't give you the steam off his piss!

One Thursday, instead of scuttling away, Al Desadora sat halfway down the bar, away from his crew. He ordered a black coffee. When she set the little dish of sugar packets next to him, he moved it an inch to the left of his coffee mug. Before he left, he asked her out for dinner.

Now, she often pictures them on that first date in a North End restaurant where the owner came to usher their waiter away to say: "For this table, there *are* no menus. Tonight, the chef and I will cook for Al Desadora and his young lady."

During that dinner, Audrey peered around at the white-cloth tables and their fellow diners —this stage-set version of the real America. Here was the real Boston, where people held up a finger to summon their waiter. She was fairly sure that nobody here had ever finagled an under-the-table cash job or slept in a creaky triple decker apartment with twice the number of legally-allowed tenants.

On their next date, just like many of her loner, afternoon bar customers, it took just two red wines for Al to start ranting on about his ex-wife. He said that, even with a big-bucks lawyer, the goddamn woman had succeeded in taking his house out from under him.

An ex-wife. Back then, Audrey had just landed from a country where divorce was still illegal, so this "ex" business felt like one more affirmation, one more bounty of this etch-a-sketch country where the past could always be erased.

That night, he invited her home for coffee and to stay over in his upstairs room where his closet and dressing table were so, so tidy.

Next morning, after a goodbye kiss, she saw that her winter coat had been moved to a new hallway hook—different from where she'd hung it.

On their third date, he asked across the restaurant table:

"You really need to wear that red nail polish? I'd prefer if you wore something classier."

Audrey bought clear nail polish. She grew out her hair bangs. She quit the Irish-American bar job. She stopped taking the south-bound Red Line T, or metro, for long, boozy nights with the girls from back home. For Valentine's, he gave her a $200 gift certificate for a huge store called Talbot's, where she bought two blouses and two pairs of tailored slacks.

On a drizzly Thursday before the Fourth of July weekend, she took the T into town, and he took an extra long lunch break to get married at Boston City Hall.

By then, they had had several more dates and sleepovers where he'd been sweet and attentive and always paid for their dinner. He'd also retitled himself Alfonsus and, a month before their wedding, he'd bought a fixer-upper cottage down on the Cape.

Poor Alfonsus, Audrey thought now, as she sat next to her husband at their usual Saturday table down at their Cape golf club. He's spent so much money on hair plugs and dental implants. But sitting here with Tom and Cecelia Webb–their usual lunch partners–he looked like a pot-bellied rabbit. And today, his transplanted hair reminded her of one of those thatch-roofed cottages they put on Irish-tourist advertisements.

Tom Webb owned a company that subcontracted for Desadora Developments. And Cecelia, with her high, squeaky voice, had once been a social worker.

Alfonsus shunted his chair closer to set his arm around his wife's shoulder. *Oh, oh. This was never good.*

"Did you hear that Miss Audrey here has been asked to volunteer at that hippie summer theater, the one down near Cedarville?"

What? Shit! Hadn't she given that kid Romney the wrong house number? Plus: she'd been so, so careful with the odometer mileage.

Alfonsus continued: "Yeah, some kid rang the house this morning while Aud was in the shower. Jesus! Those damn nonprofits. They pay zero taxes, but always with the begging bowl out. That place is a shithole anyways. Mark my words: Two years from now, it'll be all condos!"

His hand on her shoulder had curled into a fist.

He said, "Hah! And, as we all know, poor Aud here wouldn't know Shakespeare from Sesame Street, would you, sweetheart?"

Street angel.

Audrey batted her free hand toward her husband. "Oh! Would you just listen to *him*, Mr. Theater AL-ficionado!"

They all laughed. Over her vodka and tonic, Cecelia flashed Audrey a rolled-eyed smile that said, *These men of ours! What can we do with them?*

These public put-downs were just Alfonsus' target practice. Later, when they were home and behind closed doors, the most vicious stuff would detonate from his pudgy-rabbit body.

House devil.

"Closed doors." That's what Jodi O'Neil, Audrey's one-time Hyannis lawyer had said. "Closed doors are exactly the problem here. When one party doesn't or won't consent or agree, the Commonwealth of Massachusetts needs you to have one of the listed grounds for a *fault* divorce. Even then, Mrs. Desadora, you have to have verified proof or witnesses."

Well, this summer, thanks to Jimmy's help and discretion, she was going to fix this.

Later that golf-club evening, Alfonsus grabbed her arm as she rushed across the driveway from the Porsche to their kitchen door. She shook him off, but inside, he ranted and screamed, including his usual threat that he'd burn this and his Boston house—plus all his Boston investment properties–to the ground before he'd lose any of it to another goddamn woman, especially some green-card Mick chick.

This time, Audrey yelled back–not because she gave a shit, but as a decoy to keep him in here in their kitchen, not out there snooping around the back or doing his usual check-up on Jimmy's landscaping work.

The weekend after their city hall marriage, he'd driven her down here to see his latest real estate find: a two-bedroom cottage with pink roses climbing up the garden trellises. The owner had died, and this place had been abandoned and locked in probate until the old woman's family finally put it on the market.

The town wouldn't let him tear it down for a new build. But over the years, he'd paid off the planning people to dispatch a crew down here to tear out the interior walls and add a second story and white, vinyl siding. A second crew cleared out the gardens and rose trellises for a giant, brick patio and outdoor kitchen that, these days, they never used. Some mornings, when she comes back from her morning beach walk, she looks up at this house and mourns that lovely cape cottage that, just like her, has been changed and shellacked into a different version of itself.

House devil.

Just after lunchtime on July 4th, Audrey tiptoed, barefoot, across their bedroom balcony. From up here she can hear the ice-cream truck jingle, curb-crawling toward its usual parking spot along the already packed beach.

Down on the patio, a young man in a crisp, caterer's shirt was wiping last night's rainfall off their outdoor bar. A girl in a matching shirt unloaded a giant bag of ice into two steel buckets, while another girl snapped the lid off a catering box—probably the cold appetizers.

The kitchen door slid open. Alfonsus, sunglasses perched on his head and in one of his nylon golf shirts.

"No spicy stuff in these, Hon?" He asked that pretty girl arranging the appetizers on an oval-shaped tray. "I know you people love your spices." He pawed at his paunch. "But they just crucify my stomach."

Audrey watched the girl's shiny ponytail swishing back and forth. "Yes, Yes. You tell me this last year and year before, and your wife, she say on the telephone last week. "She say, 'No spices for Mister Desadora.'"

Check her watch. Two thirty. The guests were invited for three, and, just like Alfonsus, she had her own set of pre-party checks.

Climbing into and out of that Peter Pan stage harness had been much easier when the house was empty and in a tank top and gym shorts. But today, her linen party dress keeps rucking up around her thighs. Well, that's why theater folks call this a dress rehearsal, right? So as the bartender rattled the ice in the cocktail mixer for Alfonsus' usual pre-party martini, she tried the harness again.

She heard car doors slam shut, the parp-parp of key fobs as

their first guests—golf club members and business associates or connections–parked along the Desadoras' white, vinyl fence.

The Webbs were on the patio—Cecilia with that tinkly voice, and Tom with that hooting laugh. At last, the whole place rang with voices and the click-clack of high-heeled sandals.

From up here, Audrey snapped a top-down photo of each chardonnay wife and each tanned husband. Afterward, if everything went to plan here, nobody could say they weren't here. Or that they didn't see or hear.

Tick-tick-click. One of the caterers was lighting up the gas barbecue. A man's voice: "Hey, Alphonsus! Where're you hiding that pretty wife today?" Audrey switched on her recorder app and set her phone on the balcony railing.

Just one, hard kick and Peter Pan goes flying.

She kicked off and flew and it all happened in slow-motion.

One head gawking up. Then another. And another. The *oh-my-God* faces. A man's mouth unhinged and dropping open. Cecelia Webb bawling.

At last, Alfonsus followed his guests' sky-ward gazes. His martini glass shattered. She saw the top of his thatched head down there as she flew right over him. He stepped around the broken glass to follow her flight path across the patio, into the woods to that oak tree where Jimmy had hooked the second toggle bolt.

Audrey kicked at that tree. As she flew back toward the house, Alfonsus followed, panting and screaming: "You bitch!

I'm gonna break your fucking mick face."

Witnesses? Evidence? She tells that lawyer inside her head.

What time's your office open tomorrow morning?

THAT NIGHT

THAT NIGHT I was waiting for Mom outside that liquor store when I had this mental fantasy that she'd come back out of there and go, "Oh, to hell with this party, Babes. Let's go back home and order a pizza."

That'd have been brilliant, 'cos with Mom's roomies always out on Saturday nights, it'd be just me and her watching Netflix and stuffing ourselves.

By the way, this February night happened just before my 11th birthday, six years ago, when I was just a kid. And we'd gone to that store on the way from the Ashmont T station, or metro, to Alifia's house, one of Mom's waitress buddies.

Anyway, Mom came out with a bottle of wine and we headed toward the party house, and that's the thing about being a kid, right? You waste it all imagining up stupid stories.

At the party house, the front door was open and here was Alifia leaning over the upstairs banister going, "Yay! It's the Shivo girl!" Then: "Oh. You actually *brought* the kid?"

By the way, 'Shivo's' just Mom's American name, and when we fly over to visit my granny in Ireland, everyone there calls her "Siobhán."

Mom went, "Oh, come on, 'Leefie. I'm way too broke for a babysitter. Lucy'll be no bother; honest."

So now you know that I'm Lucy, not "Babes." And look, you could've plopped that February party into a different apartment, a different city, a totally different country. And you'd get the same six packs and vodka spritzers and everyone going wah-wah-wah over the crap music.

Upstairs, I ordered Mom to go find the food 'cos I was starving. But Alifia shouted to this other girl, "Hey, Amber, the Shivo girl's here!" Amber came and hugged Mom and said it was awesome, *totally awesome*. I pushed on to find the kitchen, but then Mom came after me and went, "Oh, come *on*! You can't be that hungry. Why don't you sit on that brown armchair over there, Babes?"

I tried to point out— *hello?*-- there were two people already *on* the armchair: a girl with short blond hair and this guy perched on the arm, his thigh overflowing the side.

Mom said, "Can we *try* to drop the attitude tonight, yeah?

Just go over and sit there and after I open this wine, I'll know where to find you. Like, *now*."

Fine. I sat on the other arm of that brown chair where that guy was trying to get someplace with that blond girl. But honestly? It was pervy how he loomed over her like a giant bird.

Speaking of birds, I had a bird's eye view—not that there was anything new to see. Like, except for everyone acting all chill as if they weren't watching exactly who was talking to whom.

I watched Mom coming back from the kitchen with two red plastic cups. She was wearing her purple tunic dress over the black, knee-length boots that, earlier, she'd lifted from the Goodwill. She handed me my drink (Coke) and went, "Hold out your hand. Surprise!" From her dress pocket she produced a paper towel of Doritos. Then she left.

My Coke was warm and not fizzy which pissed me off. And that fat guy just kept going on and on about his job, while that blond girl kept eyeing the living room door and checking her phone. *Bro, you don't stand a chance here,* I wanted to warn him, but, hey, it was his life, right?

Back then—like, when I was a kid–there was this other party thing. Mom'd be talking and laughing with her buddies, right?

Then one by one, or two by two, the guys would move toward her. I loved guessing which one would win.

That night, my money was on this one guy with black spiky hair who was standing with his buds near the boarded-up fireplace. Every five minutes or so, the head swiveled 'round. And

... action! He departed his flock to head toward the kitchen, where right in his path stood (surprise!) Shivo.

I watched him ask her something. She smiled. Yeah, she was interested. He said something else. Walked on. Doubled back to say something new. Above that purple dress, she tilted back her head and laughed. Spiky Hair left again, but a few minutes later, he was back and refilling Mom's glass from a new wine bottle.

Yap, yap, yap. He set his free hand on the wall just above her head. His spread-out fingers looked like a starfish. Mom had her best "oh-that's-super-interesting" face on. By now, she probably had her wine voice on, too—as in, she sounded more Irish.

That blond girl in the armchair glanced up from her phone and went, "Hey! Is that actually your mother?"

"Yeah."

She checked that living room door again. "Are you guys, like, *Irish* or something?"

"Yeah, something."

Like I said, I've actually been to Ireland. Every Christmas, even when Mom's lost her job or had a bad waitressing week, 'cos she says Granny would have a fit if we didn't go.

We fly to London, then catch a different plane to this little airport where Mom said some sort of religious stuff is supposed to have happened, like ghosts or something. When we walk out into the pitch-dark morning, there's Mom's brother, Uncle Tony, waiting for us in his car.

At Granny's house and down at the village pub, Mom

becomes Siobhán again and, for the first day or two, it's like, *who are they talking to?*

In Ireland, Mom also becomes a restaurant manager, not a food server, and she says it's impossible to get decent staff and nobody wants to work anymore, so we can't stay long. She sneaks me a sly look, like, *don't you dare rat me out here, Babes.*

The day after Saint Stephen's Day, AKA, 'Boxing Day,' we stuff the Christmas pressies into our backpacks, and Uncle Tony drives us back to that airport where Mom checks us in and goes, "Well, that's *that* over for another year, Babes."

That dude on the armchair was still talking when the blond girl got up and just walked off. I grabbed her empty seat. He shot me a killer look, like, as if something was my fault here.

Then he left, too, which was totally fine with me.

Someone brought around more tortilla chips. Then, it all turned extra boring. I thought I'd ask Mom for her phone so I could pass the time, but by now, she and Spiky Hair had grabbed one of the two window sills, where they sat thigh-to-thigh, whispering. I stayed in that brown chair until I fell asleep.

When I woke, someone had knocked over the living room floor lamp and all the wah-wah voices seemed to be in the kitchen now. The Doritos had made me super thirsty, so I went to find something new to drink—oh, and, of course, to find my mother. The fallen lamp made the light in that room weird, so I almost tripped over some girl's foot. The girl was sitting,—legs stretched out and slumped against the wall, just outside the kitchen doorway.

"Oh! Hi! So who're you, Sweetie?" She blinked at me, then reached for the red plastic cup on the floor next to her, but it was already empty.

"I'm Lucy. Shivo's daughter. Shivo *Moran,*" I added, though honestly, she was so shit faced, I don't know why I even bothered.

"Oh, that Irish girl, yeah. Hadn't seen her for ages until tonight. We once worked at a really crap restaurant together."

She looked around that living room. "So, like, where's Shivo now?"

"Mom's in the kitchen," I said.

She blinked, then blinked again. "Wait! Did you say you're actually Shivo's *kid*?"

She reached up to grab my hand like I was supposed to help her up, when all I wanted was some more of that Coke and find my Mom and get the last T home.

"Where's your Dad? Is *he* here? Like, I know he's not *here*, here. But is he still around Boston?"

"Actually, my father lives in Florida."

Now, I know what you're thinking here. And no, I actually *didn't* hear how lame I sounded. But that's the other thing about being a kid, isn't it? You spend so much time sounding *and* acting totally ridiculous, until one day you look back, and it's like, *could someone pass the puke bucket?*

When I was little I used to draw me and Mom in the park or over at Carson Beach. I hoped Mom'd put my drawings on the fridge, just like I saw at my after-school sitter's house. But Mom was always too busy getting ready for work or already gone to notice anything.

One day, I drew in a man, with an arrow pointing at his head. "Dad," I wrote, 'cos I thought that would make her say something.

Later that night, when she came home from work, she woke me up in our double bed. She handed me a photo of her younger self, with her hair in a ponytail and wearing a red sundress. Two guys, both tanned and in swimsuits, stood next to her. They were on a pale sandy beach with palm trees in the background.

I knew that Mom had left Ireland to work at a vacation resort down in Florida. But I was actually born up here, about a year after she'd moved north to Boston.

"Go on, Babes," she said. "Pick out the one who's your Dad!"

I pointed at the blond guy with a cheeky smile.

Mom clapped. "Yay! Good job! His name's Hervé. He's from Montréal, Canada, the country just above us."

Hervé. I really loved how it sounded and, as I got older, I decided I would pick a middle school where they taught French, not Spanish.

"Hervé," I said now, to that drunk girl at the party. "That's my Dad's name."

"Oh- *kaaay*. Well, you Irish always *have* to tell *some* big story."

She gave a shitty laugh--like, *ha-ha-ha*— and she actually dragged on my hand, like ringing a bell. But I wasn't going to help her up now.

In the kitchen, I ducked under people's arms and tapped people's backs to ask if they'd seen my Mom—all while, inside me, a creepy voice wondered, *Could she and that guy have left without me?*

That drunk girl came waddling across the kitchen to stand by the kitchen sink whispering to Alifia, the girl whose party it was.

No Coke, but on top of the gas stove, I found someone's half-finished can of Red Bull. I was just bringing my drink back to my brown armchair when I heard this one guy going, "Who *is* that kid?"

"It's Shivo's," said that drunk girl. She loud-whispered,

"Must've been that Irish dude she was bagging, back when we worked at that place out in Brighton. I mean, the age fits and she looks just like him."

When I pushed in that door next to the kitchen, the room smelled salty and weird, and I spotted Mom's stolen black boots standing next to the bed.

"Mo- *om*? We need to go home now," I said.

A man's voice: "Aw, for Chrissakes!"

Mom and I only had an hour to wait until the 5:15 morning train. I was really starving now, so we walked back toward the T station where, just past that liquor store, we found a McDonald's.

I'd just bitten into my egg McMuffin when she leaned across and went, "Right. Let's have it. What's got up your nose *now*?"

Back in that bedroom, as that spikey haired guy tried to find his jeans, Mom'd buttoned her purple dress up all wrong. But in McDonald's I wasn't going to tell her that.

"Give me your phone so I can listen to some music," I said.

"Like, seeing as you won't get me *my own* phone."

"Not until you tell me what this latest round of attitude is for."

I said it really, really loud, as if all those waiting customers, most of them construction workers in their high-vis yellow jackets, had come into that McDonald's just to hear me: "My Dad lives somewhere in Boston, not Florida. Not Montréal. Or maybe he's gone back home to Ireland, and he lives in County …"

You know what's extra pathetic here? Right then, if she'd held her cool and poker-faced lied to me, I'd have dropped the whole who's-my-Dad shit and gone back to believing what I'd always believed.

But across that table, she turned all twitchy scared.

She said, "Like where, Babes? So you think that *you* can tell *me* where your Dad lives now, yeah?"

In a totally cringe-y, babyish voice I said, "A woman at the party said I look just like this Irish boyfriend you had."

At last, Mom handed over her phone–probably so I wouldn't ask or say anything else.

Now, whenever I think of that party or that morning in McDonald's, I see it as that time when my mother and I put up our imaginary borders between us. We each put up silent signs saying: "This is all me and mine, not you or yours."

Man on the Train

"I TOLD you I could've walked or taken a taxi," Lorna says from the car's passenger seat. That clenched jaw, the up-tilted chin. Ouch. Yep. Her sister Eileen is really vexed at having to leave her house-party fundraiser to drive little-sis Lorna to the Waverly train station.

A half hour ago, just as two caterers carried platters of appetizers from Eileen's kitchen, Lorna's iPhone beeped from the temp nursing agency. The agency woman said that someone had called in sick again for his emergency-room shift at Boston General Hospital. So could Lorna work tonight's three swing shift?

It's New Year's Day, and even the Americans take that as an official holiday, so the agency has to pay her double time and, God knows, Lorna needs the bloody cash.

Eileen reverses around the back of the house to straighten up the car. She says: "Lorna, I really wish you'd follow up on the leads Peter and I have given you. You can't tell me it's that hard to find a permanent nursing job around here. I mean, throw a stone into Boston and you'd hit a bloody hospital."

When she's annoyed, Eileen Walsh Barrington drops the quasi-American twang and regresses to full Irish.

The sisters drive past the lit-up dining room where, through the French doors, Lorna can see the guests—huddles of board members and donors to the Waverly Town Museum where Eileen volunteers.

After the two stone pillars, Eileen turns right onto the public road toward the MBTA commuter train station.

Two months ago, November, Lorna Walsh moved here from Malawi to Boston's North Shore. Her married sister's guest bedroom, the temp agency nursing gigs—both were supposed to have been a reprieve, a sort of seaside convalescence after another year of working for "Health4All," an American-run NGO and her employer for the past 11 years.

She hasn't been issued her next overseas assignment. She cannot get herself to email or leave yet another voice message at Health4All's Washington DC headquarters to ask why and where and when. Neither can she motivate herself to log onto Eileen's computer to apply for a Boston job or, for that matter, look for a flat share in the city. So here she sits in the Lexus passenger seat, her backpack on her lap like a child being driven to school.

Lagos. Harare. Mekelle. The clinic in Malawi.

Earlier, when Eileen and Peter introduced her ("This is my sister; our globe-trotting Mother Teresa"), she tried to answer their friends' questions and comments.

"Oh, we just *loved* Africa," gushed one woman. "Cape Town is just so beautiful."

Now, Eileen's chin is lowered, so today's big-sister martyr stunt is over as they pass some dry-stone walls and off-road avenues to other huge houses perched on the rocks over the Atlantic Ocean.

In Lorna's overseas assignments, everything always felt strange at first, but three days after she'd unpacked her rucksack in a Spartan room, things always turned comfortable and familiar.

But America is too big, too cold. The trees against the sky, the antique Waverly houses and shops and town library–they're all drawn in high definition or sharp relief, like the illustrations in a glossy children's book. Here, there's a constant scrim between her and the world, and, except for the night sky from the hospital windows, she has neither seen nor been in the city of Boston.

Maybe it's not America. Or Waverly. Maybe it's her, Lorna Walsh, a 38-year-old woman who was born to live her life drifting between places and countries.

Last week, just before Lorna left for *that* temp shift, they set Eileen's iPad on the kitchen counter to Skype with Mam and their brothers back home in County Mayo. Amid all the family's jokey blather, Mam pushed her face right up to the screen.

"Lorna, *a Stór*, you're losing too much weight over there. *Musha, a Leana,* sure you're thinner now than when you were abroad in them foreign countries."

In America, in *this* foreign country, I'm the wasting-away spinster, Lorna thinks now, as they drive past a white Colonial house with a red front door. I'm a 38-year-old Miss Havisham who, when I'm not working my nocturnal shifts, I'm sitting in my seaside guest room pining for my man.

"The man" here is Stefan, an anesthesiologist with whom she first worked in Lago, then who also turned up in Mekelle.

Stefan, she suspects, is behind those un-answered calls and her Health4All assignment that hasn't come through.

"Reckon you'll be busy tonight?" Eileen asks. The face has softened; the jaw has unclenched.

"Probably. It was a pure madhouse last night. Wouldn't be New Year's Eve without your usual burns, fractures, two kids with alcohol poisoning. A car crash. Jesus! They brought in this one fella from a half-way house somewhere."

"Overdose?" Eileen asks, the face animated because, for all her suburban primness, she loves her younger sister's real-life episodes of *E.R.* So Lorna saves up the goriest or craziest of hospital tales, doling them out as siblings' peace offerings.

"No. Listen to this! So this poor fella and his pal decide to knot a load of bedsheets together, make them into a kind of rope ladder so one of them can escape from the second floor and go and buy cigarettes at an all-night petrol station. They opened the window, and the pal lowered the other guy down.

Lorna adds: "Yeah. Just one problem, though. The fella holding the rope was this scrawny little thing, the size of a blackbird, while the lad climbing down must've been 20 stone weight if he was a pound. Thwack! The sheets rip, and it's a bloody miracle he only smashed his left ankle."

Eileen thumps the steering wheel and gives a cackling laugh.

"Jesus, you were always feckin' brilliant at the stories. Just like Daddy. He'd tell a yarn and he'd have you wetting yourself laughing. Remember, Lonnie?"

Lonnie. Her childhood nickname—back when she and Eileen were both kids and their father was still alive, and when life was something you could touch and hold.

The Lexus bumps over a set of railroad tracks and then, a few hundred yards on, they turn into the train station's car park which today, is empty because nobody but Lorna Walsh is going to work on New Year's.

"You don't have to stay, Eileen. I'll be grand."

"Lonnie, stop. I'm not leaving you waiting here in the cold. Peter can hold the fort back there for a while."

Through the windshield the sisters watch an airplane, a silver dot in the winter blue sky. Eileen hits a button to open the car window to that flinty smell from the nearby salt marsh-es. Lorna feels the sour burp of sorrow.

These days, except for those middle-of-the-night texts from former colleagues in various time zones, those Health4All assignments and her one-time friends feel like a fading version of herself.

But not the Mekelle job. Lorna Walsh's big mistake was to let that Ethiopian hospital extend its borders to someplace else.

No. The real mistake happened when she let a man like Stefan walk across the shadowy hospital quad to tiptoe into her room and bed.

"I was thinking," Eileen breaks their silence. "And, Lonnie, please don't take this the wrong way. But I was thinking that you should see someone. Like, my friend Natalie sees a brilliant therapist; I could ask her if sh—"

"—Have to go." Lorna nods toward the single headlight between the winter trees as the MBTA train shunts into the tiny station.

"Thanks again!" She shouts back through the car's open door. "I hope you get all your guests to cough up lotsa bucks!"

A tall man in a brown leather jacket moves his backpack and himself closer to the window to make room for her. Opposite, across the Formica table, sit a mother and a little girl. The child, about six, spells out each letter in the station name: "W-A-V …"

Lorna looks through the open door to the next carriage.

What the hell? This afternoon, the in-bound train is absolutely jammers–packed.

When she unzips her puffy coat, Lorna accidentally elbow jabs her seat neighbor. "Sorry. I thought it'd be empty today. Thought everyone'd be at home staying warm."

"Oh, Wow! Is that an Irish accent I'm hearing?"

She's not in the mood for the follow-on questions about what county and when and why she immigrated here—especially when, in fact, she hasn't. "Yes."

Silence. No follow-on questions from this bloke who smells of fresh timber and seems accustomed to scrunching himself into too-small places. When he shifts in his seat, he brushes her knee under their table.

An electronic voice announces the next station. The child across from them spells out this station name, too.

Lorna's phone beeps. Probably another Health4All buddy wishing everyone a Happy New Year. *Don't. Don't check your iPhone to see if it's Stefan.*

Yep, it's a group text from Rhina, who now works at a hospital in Sidney. Rhina says she's been away in Taz on a holiday; otherwise she'd have wished everyone a Happy New Year earlier.

People start texting back their emoji's and "same to you, Rhina sweetie."

Lorna looks up to catch the man peering over her shoulder.

"Off out on a night on the town?" He asks, a diversion from being caught prying.

"Going to work, actually."

"Oh. No fun."

"I'm a nurse."

He pats the overstuffed backpack on his lap. "I'm going ice skating. I'm sure you heard. The city's waiving all fees for the Frog Pond for the next two weekends. Part of the mayor's 'stay-cation in our own city' thing."

Is Lorna supposed to respond, to say something new here?

He nods toward the train's luggage racks stuffed with puffy coats and ice skates peeping from tote bags. "Looks like all these folks heard about the freebie, too."

Outside, the winter light is waning beyond the trees and houses and power lines.

"Party hearty to ring in the New Year last night?"

"Nope. I had to work last night, too." In her mind's eye, she sees that chap, the one who climbed out a half-way-house window, his ankle all bandaged up as he squinted from his hospital gurney at her. "You know," he'd said. "You're a real sweetheart."

She'd wanted to contradict that patient, to tell the truth—just like her late father had taught her. *No I'm not. Not a sweetheart.*

The train guy cuts across her thoughts. "I didn't go out either. This New Year's Eve thing—too many happy or *pretend-*

happy people. Too many"—He makes air quotes between them—'circus animals all on show.'"

Wait. A man in a worn leather jacket, a man who smells like wood shavings, is quoting W.B. Yeats to her?

Shite. Did I just think, say that? Christ. I'm turning into my sister. "Yeats—W.B. himself," he says, as if he's read her thoughts.

"One of your countrymen?" He folds his arms, stretches back

against the train seat. "Old W.B. was right, though. Half of us are just going through the motions, especially around the holidays."

In for a penny. I'll never see this man again anyway. He's the proverbial stranger on the train.

"Yeah. It's been, well ..." Trying for wry humor, she mimics his air quotes. "'The winter of my discontent.'"

"Discontent? Geez. That's kinda rough. Can I ask your name?"

"Lorna. Lorna Walsh."

"Ken. Ken Brown—the third." He extends a handshake. "I'm a boat builder—well, boat *restorer*. Work on two-masted fishing schooners–the original cod-fishing boats around these parts. Not much call for boat repairs this time of year, so I do some indoor carpentry work. I play a few music gigs when I can get them. Go ice skating." He nudges her. "That's all when I'm not straight-out busy reciting Yeats to pretty girls on trains!" *Piss off.*

He catches her nettled look. "Sorry. Honest. I'm not trying to be sketchy."

"No. No. It's not. I mean, you're not." *What does 'sketchy' actually mean?*

She maneuvers toward the seat edge. He moves further toward the train window. The train slows. The electronic voice announces. Lorna braces herself for the kid's new spelling tryout. More passengers troop past her seat with their tote bags and backpacks and children's runny noses.

Ken Brown has propped his elbow on the window ledge. There, in the dusty window, overlaid against some graffiti-d warehouses, Lorna sees dislocated bits of her and this American man, this boat-builder, muddled and mirrored among the train's reflected lights.

"Nobody's happy all the time," he says. "I don't know how long you've lived over here, but in this country we just *think* we should." He makes another air quote. 'Life, liberty and the pursuit of happiness.' Blah, blah, blaaaah."

"Chelsea!" Drones the announcement voice. "Chelsea Station next. Then *North* Station, Boston."

"Goodbye, then," Lorna says at North Station, standing there in the train looping her arms into her backpack straps. "Enjoy your ice-skating."

She's branching right toward the station's exit doors when she feels a hand on her arm.

Wait!" he says. "Jeez. You really *are* a nurse. Nobody else walks this fast."

"Look, I have to get to work." He overtakes her, blocks her path toward the door and stands there with his arms spread. "Oh, come on! I think you and I need to hang out this evening. You could call in sick. I mean, you are, right? Sick? You told me yourself." He mimics someone writing on a prescription pad, "Doctor Brown here is officially diagnosing you with Seasonal Defective Disorder."

"It's ' *affective* disorder'." She detours around him and out the station's double doors.

He catches up with her again as she waits for the crosswalk sign on the corner of Staniford and Lomasney Way. A woman in a scarlet red puffer coat waits next to them.

"Only one cure," he says, out of breath as they stand elbow to elbow. "Only one cure for what you've got, my friend." *Oh, Christ. So he's* one of those *eegits* who equates a train conversation with a screen swipe on a Tinder app?

The woman in the red coat takes a few steps to the left, then jaywalks out into the traffic, probably to avoid them.

Lorna lunges at him, her fist stopping just before his jaw.

"Listen, I'm *not* your friend. I'm *not* tonight's ride or pick-up for you. What the hell is wrong with you damn men?"

Ken backs up, arms raised in surrender. "Whoa! Whoa! Please. I don't know who these 'damn men' of yours are, and yeah, maybe you should go take a swipe at them—or *him.* Look, I'm just a guy inviting you to come ice skating with me. If you hate it you can leave after 10 minutes, and we'll never see each other again. If you love it, call up Mayor Wu and thank her for her freebie."

The walk-sign appears. He hoists his backpack higher and crosses ahead of her, then turns up the sloping footpath on Staniford Street.

From the doorway of the take-away burrito place, Lorna calls in a sickie to the temp agency. The woman listens to only half of Lorna's sick lie, then sighs and hangs up.

Google Maps guides her across Cambridge Street and between the red-brick houses on Beacon Hill. As she walks, she pictures that agency woman deleting her from the database. Oh, well. There are other agencies. Other hospitals.

She waits for the light to change before crossing to the concrete stairs down to Boston Common, where the bare winter trees are all strung with sparkly blue lights.

At the pond, he's whizzing around, towering over everyone else and wearing what looks like a child's teddy-bear-styled hat with dangling ties and two black-and-white eyes peering from the front.

In her rented skates, she hangs onto the sides of the rink.

She trudges, not glides, a few more feet while, across the rink, all those families and teens and kids keep skating under the strung up lights. Step. Step. At this rate, it's going to take her all night just to make it around. Christ! An emergency room shift is 50 times easier than this shite.

Another step. Another. *OK. I got this. Now, step away, hands off.* She scrabbles wildly at the air before tumbling backward onto her arse. She sits, winded and sore. Has she splintered her tail bone here? Two skating teens separate to maneuver around her, then, laughing, they hold hands again.

The tears come, trickling down her frozen cheeks. Once she starts, she just can't stop.

He's suddenly crouched next to her, the faux animal eyes

staring from that hat. "Here, my friend. Just grab my arm. You're going to be OK. I promise."

Lorna clutches his forearm. He holds steady, then rises, ever so slowly, while she holds on.

SNOW

I WAS JUST ABOUT to lock up for the night when a man's face appeared between the flyers and leaflets pasted on the shop door. It was Mr. Ferguson, that Dubliner who'd just bought our village *ostán*, or hotel, across the street.

He pushed in the door; a tanned face and the hair and shoulders dotted from our late-afternoon snow shower.

"Just today's *Times* and a packet of mints," he said at the checkout counter. He asked in English, not *Gaeilge* or Irish, which made me happy.

Over in the butcher area, in her blue shop coat with my father's surname– *Ó Catháin*–stitched over the pocket, Bríd's ritual cleaning turned much louder. She's never liked blow-ins or tourists, and this hotel investor was and would bring both.

"Congratulations, Mr. Ferguson!" I said, nodding through the front window toward the three-story hotel with years' worth of green damp weeping down the front walls. "I really hope it works out for you ..."

Bríd coughed.

"Oh, thanks very much," Mr. Ferguson said. "Bit of a *kip*, but I just sold two places down on the Spanish *Costa*, and the price was right down here. Oh, and … Declan's the name. All the 'misters' in this country died off years ago."

"Dolores," I said. When we shook hands, he held on a second too long.

"By that twang of yours, I'd say you're home from the States, yeah? Where are you and what are you doing over there?"

In the three weeks since I landed back here, nobody—the shop customers, Bríd, and certainly not my father upstairs in his sick bed—have inquired about a life or a job in America.

"We're in Tanberry, just outside Boston; we call it 'the south shore.'"

Bríd gave another of her prudish little coughs, which only made me lean further over that checkout counter. "I'm a buyer for a commercial construction company. The guys on the crews say that I know more about sheetrock and ceiling tiles than most of them."

His eyebrows rose. "Jeez. Well, now I *am* impressed. Listen, I've a load of samples over there for the rooms. You might want to come over and take a gander. The woman's touch and all that." He paused. "Like, if you're hanging around here for a while, yeah?"

I wished I could answer that question. I wished I could say,

"Tomorrow. Actually, I'm flying from Shannon tomorrow."

I walked him back to the shop door, then stood watching this man crossing our village street, the folded newspaper held over his head against the falling snow.

Twenty-three years ago, Bríd, who's my late Mother's first cousin, came to this house to help my father and 11-year-old me to get ready for the funeral and to organize my mother's funeral tea. The tea was held across the street in the hotel lounge, but I don't remember her funeral and, of course, I haven't been inside that hotel since.

Afterward, my father took the black mourning scarf from our front door, and gave Bríd the shop job. So here she still was now, keeping shop and cleaning and yapping to the neighbors.

Three weeks ago, when she rang across the Atlantic, I thought that the kitchen phone was part of my night dream.

Murph, my American husband, got up to grab it. In bed, he handed me the receiver and, there, suddenly, was Bríd's voice.

"It's your father, Séamus," she shouted, as if I'd forgotten my father's Christian name, and as if the shouting would shorten the miles and years between us. Then, in a blather of Irish, she told a long, rambling story of how the doctor had warned him, begged him, even put him on blood pressure tablets and told him to eat better and go for a walk every day. "But sure, you know your father," she said.

Oh, yes. I knew my father—even if we hadn't talked for over 20 years. She said that Séamus was carrying a side of beef out of the back-room cooler when the heart finally got him, and thank God she was still there to ring the ambulance.

Later, I stood under our *en-suite* shower where I realized that I'd never actually inquired about the cardiologist's prognosis. Later still, when Murph had left for work, I sat at our kitchen counter browsing the Aer Lingus website. One inner voice said not to bother, while another voice said that I owed my own father a sick-bed visit.

Next morning, the airport doors slid open to Bríd's husband Seán standing there at Shannon Airport. It was just gone six o'clock, Irish time, and Seán looked much older and craggier than I remembered.

After the airport, the lorries and cars and the green motorway signs made me feel like I was moving through one of those immersive art exhibits where everything is there, but not real.

I must have dozed, because the sun was up as Seán exited off the motorway to take another roundabout and, eventually, to turn in the hospital gates. In the parking lot, he said he'd have a bit of a sleep while I went into that city hospital to see my father.

By now, the cars outside the next-door pub were covered, and the snow was making halos around the village street lights. The shop closed up for the night, I'd come outside to take the broom to the front steps.

"Sure ye must be used to this carry on," Bríd called back from the village footpath. In her black puffer coat, she was headed home for the night.

"I saw them there on the telly one night in New York. Big machines and ploughs and the devil knows what. You wouldn't see the likes of it in Siberia!"

I said, "Oh, this is just a dusting, Bríd. Back *home* it's nothing to get six or twelve inches, and that's just in one storm."

Underneath the fur-trimmed coat hood, she frowned at that word–home. Then she started to pick and skid her way up the village footpath toward her own home.

Some nights, in the four-bedroom house that I designed and Murph built, I still dream *as Gaeilge*. I never remember those dreams' plots or scenes, but Murph nudges me awake because, he says, I sound like I'm calling out for someone lost.

"Who?" He used to ask, in our younger, sweetheart days, back when I stayed over at his dingy bachelor flat up in Quincy. "Just tell me that Irish asshole's name you keep calling for, and I'll go chase him down–oh yeah, in the middle of the night!" He'd laugh at his own joke. Murph is good at laughing.

Upstairs, my father sat propped against his pillows, his chin rolled forward, asleep, while a British comedy blared from the small television on his dressing table.

He still kept to his left-hand side of this double bed, as if my mother were about to creak across the landing to lie in next to him. I touched his shoulder. He started awake.

These were the eyes that met me that morning when, creaky with night-flight exhaustion, I turned from the florescent-lit corridor into his hospital ward.

"Daughter," I mimed at the nurse in her blue scrubs, pointing at myself. She smiled and crossed to the bed to touch his shoulder. "Mister O Catháin! Look! A very nice surprise, a visitor for you!"

He lay there, staring, as if I'd just stepped off a spaceship.

The nurse asked how he was feeling today. He answered in English. Then, he shot that nurse a sly look before switching to rapid-fire Irish: "Well, would you just look at who it is? The returned *poncán*, or Yank. Well, I hope you have a return ticket with tomorrow's date on it, *a chailín*. 'Cos if it's the business and my money that brought you back, you can forget it."

Now, he flattened his legs for me to set the tea tray on the bed, and he nodded toward the window and the snow falling outside. "Did you sweep the snow off the front steps?"

As I crossed to close the bedroom curtains, I answered in English because I wouldn't bloody gratify him, and because, with a man like my father, you use whatever you've got.

On his first night home from the hospital, I woke up in my girlhood bedroom where the walls were lined with cardboard boxes of washing powder and Corn Flakes—supplies for the shop downstairs. I lay there listening for his step-step to the toilet. Nothing. I got up and crossed the landing to his door, but now that we were out of the hospital and back in the house and village, I couldn't just go in there for no reason, or without permission.

Push in the goddamn door, I told myself as I stood on the landing, in a wedge of brightness from the village street light. Five, six, seven minutes before I rattled the knob and shoved the door open.

"What?"

"I ... hadn't heard you. I got worried."

"Oh, for Jayzus' sake," he roared into the empty space between us.

Now, I shouted over the bedroom telly: "D'you want anything else?"

"I wouldn't feed this to cattle," he answered, through a mouthful of buttered toast. High fiber. Sodium free. I'd ordered it, specially, from a baker in Galway. He washed it down with a slug of tea.

For days now, I've wanted to lean in and howl into his old face: A goddamn thank-you would be nice, some appreciation for leaving my house, my husband, our business ... And look at me when I'm speaking to you!

"Awesome!" I said, sweeping a few toast crumbs off the duvet cover. "Sure, knock if you need something."

In the front parlor, I plugged in the electric fire that he'd installed in the old fireplace. I could still hear that television comedy while, across the street, an upstairs light got switched on in the hotel. I saw a dark figure–Declan Ferguson on a fold-able step ladder, his crotch level with the window sash. A green light shade just beyond his right shoulder. Weren't the hotel light shades always green? Yes, they were. I remembered.

In my early days in America I told cute Irish stories about neighbors and drinkers and men saving hay in the fields and, sometimes, I told about that morning when the hallway phone rang from the hospital with the news of my dead mother. From that story, I hopscotched forward to those later, post-funeral scenes where huddles of head-scarved women stood smoking and gossiping around the shop checkout. They fingered my long hair and said that I was such a grand little *cailín*, and such a *sólás*, a comfort to my poor widowed father.

At age 11, how could I have known that you can never comfort a man who rages at the world and everything that the world has done to him? And, now that I've flown back here, how can I comfort a man who still hasn't forgiven me for leaving for America?

Every Christmas, when I came home on holidays from my teenage boarding school outside Dublin, our two village pubs were always packed with young men back from England, flashing the cash and sinking pints, telling silly English stories and, in my father's version of it, 'bringing even more shame on their family.'

"Nobody in our family ever had to 'take the boat,'" he used to say across our kitchen table. And then, one day, I finished boarding school and started—but then quit—my Dublin college to depart for what was supposed to have been a summer in

America. Ever since, my mailed, "Merry Christmas" cards have gone unanswered. Ditto for my transatlantic phone calls.

Now, my cell phone rang from where I'd left it next to that old mantel clock above the fireplace. Murph. Phone to my ear, I went back to my spot inside the front window.

"Left work early, Hon," he said. "Only gone two over here, but we already have three or four inches, with more coming tonight. The snow plows were out all the way up Route 24."

I could hear him snapping a can open as he went to fill the dog dish for Hilda, our four-year-old golden retriever. When Murph called, I always wished myself back there, in my own kitchen and home. But for the past few nights, I've felt impatient with his check-ins—as if there was something more important for me here.

"Miss you babe," he said now, while, across the village street, Declan Ferguson stretched his arms out to measure the top of that hotel window. "Hilda keeps looking for your car in the driveway. Oh! And the girls in the office all say 'hello.'"

How could Ferguson *not* have heard the hotel door open and shut? Or my snow-slushy steps across the tiled lobby, where I stopped to peer into the hotel lounge with its old, flowery carpet and all the stools upturned on the banquettes and tables?

In the bar, he swiveled around on his high stool. Mouth dropped open in fake, staged surprise.

"Jeez, Dolores! I wasn't expecting any visitors on a night like tonight. But here, take a seat. A drink. I've no wine or beer. Just spirits, but no ice or mixers."

I leaned in to see the giant book spread open on the counter.

"Your samples? Nice stuff!"

"Ah, keeping at it. I've a crew in Dublin I can take off another job. Get them down here and at least half the rooms ready before the Easter Bank Holiday weekend. But here, love, take off your coat. Wouldn't put a bleedin' dog out."

He held my gaze, then looked away, then looked back again, as if to verify what he'd already guessed—or knew.

"So, you're probably used to this weather," he said. "Winters are supposed to be pure brutal over there. Don't know how you stand it. Or are you into the skiing? Yeah? A buddy of mine went skiing over there last year. Someplace near a lake in Cali-fornia, I think. Jeez, no. I'll take th'oul sun holiday any day. Sun, sea and sand and a few rounds of golf and tapas and a good cabernet and Declan here is happy out!"

"Oh, you get used to it," I said. "Two years ago, the snow banks were nearly as high as our gutters." I stretched my left arm all the way up, willing him to spot or ask about my wedding band, to protect me from my raging, crazy self.

From a shelf behind the bar came a sudden burst of radio static, then an RTÉ radio announcer introducing a nighttime concerto.

Declan Ferguson and I had finished our second drink when I raised my voice over that radio music to say: "I ... I really should go. Don't know if you heard, but I'm taking care of my father. He might need someth–"

"—Ah! Stop! Sure, where would you be off to in this bleedin' weather?" His voice was velvety with cognac and cocked sureness.

Upstairs, he led me to a hotel room with a green light shade and where his overnight duffle bag sat unzipped in the corner of the room. I walked around the bed to the window where I could see my footprints in a diagonal path from my father's front door to here.

Behind me, the bed creaked. I was supposed to turn around now, to give a foxy smile before I joined him there.

In bed we blathered on, boozy words rising and floating while, out that window, I watched the snow still making haloes around the village street light.

When Ferguson rose above me, I saw myself down there, in that lounge just beneath this room. A prim, precocious kid in a gray cardigan over a tartan skirt, my black patent shoes scuff-scuffing along the carpet as I went from table to table, asking each funeral mourner if they'd like another sausage roll.

That girl, my memory of her. Not concocted or imagined. I knew that because, there, in that hotel bed, as Declan Ferguson moved inside me, tears tracked down my cheeks and now I knew, finally, that I hadn't flown back here for my father.

Afterward, Ferguson flopped over onto his back, then patted my shoulder. "Janey. Are you all right? Aw, Christ.! Look, we can't have you crying here. You better stay the night." He patted my shoulder again until his tanned face softened into sleep.

I pushed in the front door to see my father up there, a pajama ghost in the landing light.

"Are you OK?" I shouted as I stamped the snow off my shoes. "Were you knocking for something?"

"You could've burned the place down over my head with that heater left plugged in like that."

His bare feet smack-smacked across the landing linoleum. His bedroom door slapped shut.

American Wake

IT WAS Uncle Vin who nicknamed my going-away barbecue, "Drey's American wake." Vin is my mother's youngest brother, the self-appointed family comedian. Once he called it that, that's how my party and the invitations got sent around in all the family texts.

My grandmother explained that this 'American wake' stuff was from history and not actually about barbecues or anybody being dead. Instead, years and years ago, that's what they used to call the party for people going to America or Canada on a ship. Of course, Granny didn't remember that herself–like, she's only 78– but she said that it had happened to her aunts and uncles and *their* aunts and uncles. All of them, like me and Gran, lived in County Mayo, and before they left, they were given an American wake where everyone brought food and wine and beer. Everyone stayed up all night until it was time to walk that person down to their bus or train that would take them to that emigrant ship. Down at the bus or train station, they all cried.

Oh wait! History is only my third favorite school subject, but even I know that it couldn't actually be a bus or train, right?

Back then, it'd have been more like a horse and cart or

something, and, in those days (Gran said), it took a whole fortnight to get to America.

Drey's just my nickname; I was christened Andrea Jane. My aunts and uncles down in County Mayo were throwing this party for me because, six months ago, my mother had left for Boston. And, now that my spring school term was nearly finished, I had to go over there to live with Mam.

By then, I'd actually been living down the country with my Granny for over six months, and I had to move from Dublin across the country to Mayo 'cos my Mam and Dad were separated and waiting for a divorce. Then, just after Halloween last year, Mam had got a nursing job over in Boston, with a sign-on bonus that sounded great. I Googled it. The hospital really looked huge.

This was the same hospital where, long before she'd ever met Dad, Mam had actually worked, so she had an American work visa and everything. Now, after years of just being Mam, she'd gone back to work to save enough money to eventually come back to Ireland to buy a new house for the two of us–oh, and for Freckle, my ginger cat.

"It's just temporary, Pet," she'd said that morning when she'd left for Dublin airport. I didn't cry that morning, and I hadn't the heart to remind her that, the year after next, I'd actually be in the university, so we wouldn't even need a house—at least not for two people. Or maybe we would. Or she would.

Anyways, the American wake party was at Gran's, and I really didn't care what they called it, so long as they didn't expect me to do the crying part.

That day was sunny, so we set up the table and a few chairs on the cement verandah outside the kitchen, where Granny and the other women sat. My younger cousins were kicking football in the garden, and a few of the other uncles went to join in, while Vin did the barbecue. Geraldine, Mam's other sister, brought a big salad with goat cheese on top. Auntie Ann, Uncle Cathal's wife, brought coleslaw and a thing with sweet potatoes, and a few of the neighbors and Mam's friends brought other stuff.

As he turned over the sausages and burgers and chicken, the more beer Uncle Vin drank, the funnier he thought he was.

Once the food was ready, he took a bite of burger and said, "Oh, yeah, Drey. That's *reeeeal* good. Uh-huh." He laughed at his own imitation of an American accent. He teased that, in no time at all, I'd be talking like a Yank, and everyone would be calling me Andrea, my full name, because the Yanks like everything A-OK. The others laughed along, but I've always found Vinnie's jokes super annoying, so I moved away from him to sit closer to the aunts and Gran.

Auntie Geraldine said that Mam was a lucky duck to have found that big-bucks job. Auntie Maura chimed in that I was going to America at just the right time, when we could be going down to Cape Cod every single weekend to get a tan. And then, added poor Auntie Helen, who's Vinnie's wife, it'd be the Christmas holidays, and I'd be landed right back to Ireland to spend the winter school break with my Dad in Dublin and they could all take a day to come up to Dublin to visit me and we'd do a bit of shopping and lunch.

Vera, who's Gran's neighbor and Mam's old school friend, interrupted to say that, actually, she didn't like America at all.

No, not one bit. Yeah, she and the kids had gone over to Disney two years back, and she was *not* impressed with that whole country.

"Or I can come down here straight after Christmas Day," I said, looking down at Freckle, who, by now, had curled up on my lap.

Just like at a real wake, they were trying to console or cheer me up—or to *cover* up what they weren't saying. Like, nobody was saying that, once, not that long ago, me and Mam and Dad and Freckle were a normal family living in a normal house in Rutlinstown, on the southside of Dublin. They weren't saying that a bank had taken back our Dublin house–plus all the half-built, unfinished housing estates that Dad's company had been building until he lost his money.

One newspaper showed a photo of one of those half-finished estates, with the windows all boarded up and a big, blue plastic thing instead of a real roof, on each of those houses.

See, Mam and her family think that they've protected me from the full story. That's very kind of them, but I'm 15 years of age, and you'd need to have absolutely no WiFi *not* to have seen all those news articles about my Dad–including that giant photo of Mam and Dad and me, at age 12, out at the helipad where we were waiting for the helicopter to the Galway horse races. We always took the helicopter because in the summer, the motorway was way too busy, and it took too long to get across the country. In the photo, Mam's dress was fluttery, and she had her hand up, holding her summer hat on her head so the wind from thèchopper blades wouldn't blow it away.

"What goes up must come down." That's what they wrote underneath that photo.

"The harder they fall." That's what another headline said. Plus, in an online business magazine I'd found, they called my Dad "a poster-boy" for Ireland's over-borrowed and over-priced housing market. I read that and I thought, Seriously?

Listen, if you saw my Dad now–who, by the way, lives in Fairview, Dublin, with his new girlfriend–you'd say he was no poster boy. Not for anything.

The only one who stayed quiet at that American wake barbecue was Granny. When I looked across the verandah, she looked really sad, and sometimes she kind of shook her head, like she couldn't really believe that all this was happening.

Back in the winter, I was actually fine with Mam leaving. I mean, it would be a break from all the phone calls and drama, and it wasn't like my mother was moving to the other side of the planet. But then, they said I had to move down here to Granny's, and change to a boring, small-town school with a super ugly uniform. In that school, I'd be sitting listening to some boring teacher, and I'd think about my mother, but I could only see one bit of her at a time. Her blond, highlighted hair. Her long, thin legs. Her smile.

Or, later, I'd be at the supermarket with Gran and I'd think that I actually saw Mam.

To see my entire mother, I had to wait for our weekly video calls, when I got to see her new, Boston apartment that was, she said, by the seaside. Behind her, on the wall of her American living room, hung a school photo of me in my Dublin school uniform.

Now, within 24 hours after that party in Mayo, I was actually going to be *in* that apartment and walking on the nearby beach. Like, for real.

Honestly, I couldn't listen to Uncle Vin's stupid jokes or look at Granny's sad face anymore. I acted like the midges were really biting my arms, and went in the house, as if I needed to get the spray stuff. Freckle came, too, and we both went upstairs to lie on top of my bed. My packed-up suitcase stood next to the wardrobe. Along the other wall of that room stood all these packing boxes full of me and Mam's stuff—like, from when we'd moved away from Dublin and Dad and our house.

I could still hear the voices downstairs and outside—the kids cheering as someone scored a football goal. Someone laughed.

Someone else scraped a few chairs—probably because it was time to move back inside. Through the gable window, I could see that the light had turned kind of gauzy grey and I could hear the pigeons hoo-hoo-hooting in the trees.

I was just nodding off to sleep when, one by one, I imagined all those packing boxes un-taping themselves. Our stuff climbed out over the sides and went downstairs and paraded across the whole country to south Dublin. Inside my head, there was my stuff, standing on the front steps to ring on our old door bell.

When the new owners answered, they said, "Excuse us, but this is actually *our* house." Then, one by one, they marched upstairs to my old room and reinstalled themselves back into their proper places.

In this Dublin part of the story, Freckle was magically back there, too—all curled up on the couch in front of the fireplace in the downstairs lounge, and yes, there was Dad sitting at the kitchen island, reading his *Times*.

Next morning, the windows were speckled with rain and the sink was full of dirty dishes and glasses and the house still smelled of charred food. I made tea for everyone and put on some toast before Auntie Maura came to drive me and Gran to the train station in Westport.

At the station, Auntie Geraldine came, too, on her way from dropping the kids off at school. Their hoods pulled up against the morning rain, Gran and the two aunts helped me load my suitcase. They hugged me. Auntie Maura slipped fifty euro into my coat pocket. Auntie Geraldine said I'd be home in no time.

Gran kept blowing her nose into one of her old-timey cotton handkerchiefs.

No crying for me. Not even as I sat there on the train, with that platform gliding behind me and the three of them still waving through the dusty, rain-dotted window. Once I couldn't see them anymore, I pulled a book out of my backpack and forced myself *not* to picture Freckle back there, mewling at her food dish.

Later, at Heuston Station, I wheeled the suitcase up the platform. Just beyond the barrier, I spotted Dad and a woman.

He had his arm around her shoulders.

"Fee- *ooooh*-nah." That's what Mam called Dad's girlfriend, always rolling her eyes as she said it. Dad looked even worse than the last time I'd seen him, Easter Monday, when he'd taken the train down to treat me to lunch in a restaurant in Westport.

Yeah, Dad. Loose the dirty baseball hat, I thought as he finally spotted me and started racing across the station.

Look, none of this was Fiona's fault. So after Dad, I hugged her, too, and Dad introduced us.

From the passenger seat of Fiona's car, Dad kept swiveling around to ask me stupid stuff, like, how was the train journey up, and how was the end of the school year and did I get good marks on my report card? I said nothing about that American wake party. Soon, Dad and I had nothing left to say.

Out my car window, Dublin was still Dublin. But kind of not Dublin, too; like, as if it could also be just some city I'd once visited.

At the airport, Fiona said she needed to buy something at a shop. Dad wheeled my suitcase toward the check-in queue for Boston. As well his shitty cap and jeans, he was kind of scrunched over, like someone's Grandad.

I remembered how, once, two years ago, when we were flying to our place in the Algarve, a woman spotted us and left her own airport queue to come up to us.

"Mr. O'Brien," that woman said. "Ah, we rang your office there last week looking for corporate sponsorship for our charity walk for the Heart Association. Can we put you down as the main underwriter again this year?" Dad told that woman that he'd get his people to take care of it.

Afterward, in the VIP airport lounge, he said to Mam and me, "Jayzus, it's not like I'm Bono or the bloody Pope. Make a few million in this country and everyone's suddenly your friend."

Fee-oooh-nah was back, but I couldn't see that she'd actually bought anything. We listened to another airport announcement, this one a boarding call for all passengers for Logan Airport, Boston.

Dad and I hugged. I pulled back first. He wiped his sleeve across his face. Fiona set a hand on his shoulder. Yep, my Dad was crying. Not me. Like I said, there was absolutely zero point.

"Going to Boston?" The woman next to me on the airplane asked.

She had a super *culchie* accent, and I've always hated people who ask questions to which there's an obvious answer. Still, I nodded and smiled—the sort of smile that said, *Please don't talk to me*.

"Here, love." She was offering a roll of Polo mints. "It's hard to fly on your own, but these are brilliant for the ears!"

"No, thank you," I said. "I've flown before. Like, loads of times, but this is my first time in coach class."

The woman made a "well-pardon-me" face, then pulled back the roll of mints. Her husband was jab-jab-jabbing at the screen on the back of his window seat. The passenger in the row in front of us turned around and said, "Excuse me, but could you please stop pushing against my seat?"

Seven hours later, our seatbelt sign dinged, and that woman's husband woke up and pushed up the window blind. I leaned over for a look. Down there, America was a stripe of land bordered by water dotted with white boats. Then, the land slid away, and the sky turned blue-er. The sun disappeared behind lots of gray buildings, between which my mother was probably rushing or sitting in a speeding taxi.

The airport was smaller than Heathrow, and a man in a suit helped me to lift my suitcase off the conveyor belt.

"Got it, Hon?" He asked as he set it on the floor beside me. I told this American man that I was fine, and then I pulled my big suitcase behind me, my backpack bopping against my back as I walked out into a line of waiting people with bunches of flowers and typed-up signs with people's names: "Stratowsky." "Ferris." "Eisner."

No Mam. In the Arrivals area, I stood there while people divided around me. I checked my phone. Shit. Had she forgotten? I texted her. Nothing. I'd give her 15 more minutes before I rang Dad to book me a room in the airport Hilton, where I presumed he still had his free rewards vouchers.

"Drey!" Mam sprinting across the airport toward me. Her hair was in a ponytail and she wore an ugly blue top over matching blue pajama trousers—her nurse's gear.

"Sorry! Sorry!" She kept saying. "One of the evening shift needed something explained in a patient's EHR, so I missed the T, and had to wait for the next one!"

As we hugged, I forgot how annoyed I was at her for being late. When she finally pulled away, her eyes were watery.

Outside, I headed toward the line of airport taxis. Wait! Where was she? She and my suitcase were still back on the footpath to the right of the airport doors. She beckoned me back there.

"We'll be grand," she said, as we climbed the steps of this silver-colored bus. "This'll be a lot more fun." Wait! Did she sound a teeny bit American already?

From our seat bus we snapped and texted a selfie of us to Granny and the aunts so they'd all know that I'd landed safely.

Next, she asked all these questions about last night's American wake party, which felt really weird. Like, how could that party in Mayo be last night when, over here, it actually felt like it was three nights or a whole week ago?

Don't ask about Dad.

She asked about Dad, and I said that he was there to collect me off the train and *he* was right on time, actually early.

She hesitated, then asked: "How ... does he look?"

"Good, yeah," I said and, of course, I didn't mention Fee-ooh-nah.

Once we left the airport, America was bits of roads and streets and big green signs and people walking along. Actually, some of the buildings in the distance looked kind of old, and nearly everyone out there on the Boston footpaths was wearing sunglasses—just like in Portugal.

After the silver bus, we had to stand on the footpath to wait for another bus. Even in those ugly nurse's clogs, I had to rush to keep up with Mam. There was no bus stop or sign, but she said this one was a free shuttle that went from her hospital to all these other clinics and a rehabilitation place.

"It's free!" She said, over her shoulder as she flashed a plastic identity badge at the driver. "Free for staff and patients!"

Before, on our other trips abroad, Dad had led the way and checked us all in and flagged down the taxis. But as we dragged my suitcase up the steps of that second bus with the hospital name on the side, I saw how she really *was* different. In Boston, Mam was the boss.

"Right, this is us," Mam said, as that hospital shuttle creaked to a stop.

We walked past lots of shops and take-aways—most with Spanish names and signs. Spanish, by the way, is sort of my second favorite school subject. Hold on. Mam'd said her place was by the sea, but where *was* the sea?

We were at a three-story house, 32 Charles Street—the address where I'd posted her birthday present and her Mother's Day card. To the right of that dirty-looking front door, I counted six black post boxes—all numbered, though the person in Number 4 hadn't collected their post in weeks, maybe months.

Inside, the front hall was dark and spooky, like one of those American movies where cops burst in, guns out and bellowing "Police! Freeze!"

On the third floor, Mam unlocked Number 6 and led the way into her living room. There, across a lot of other house roofs and between two big chimneys, was the sea.

Mam started to ask me something, but right then, an airplane was outside the window, heading right toward her flat. It was super loud and looked like it really could crash into that house. Once it was gone, I crossed to her living room window. Down there, way over to the right and across a bit of harbor, I saw these ugly buildings—the airport I'd just landed in.

Underneath Mam's windowsill stood a small, white table with a laptop. Without turning around, I knew exactly what I'd see on that opposite wall—that framed photo of me in my old school uniform.

Stupid me. On our transatlantic video calls, I had filled in the rest of the picture to imagine up a really cool, open-plan apartment with white leather couches and a straight-on view of a sandy beach. Not this little room with its cheap, brown carpet and only one armchair that looked, like that white table, all charity shop.

In her living room, Mam pulled that blue nurse's top over her head and stepped out of those blue pajama pants. "I'm actually not supposed to wear these outside the hospital, but I was in a rush," she said, as she walked, in her knickers and bra, toward her bedroom where there was a window cut into the slanted roof.

"Ok, where's *my* room?" I asked.

She bent to tug at something beneath her single bed. It clicked and here, sliding out, was a slat of wood with a skinny mattress on it. "It's a trundle bed! I found it at a garage sale! We'll put your sheets and duvet on later."

Her face was flushed—probably from the awful heat in that bedroom. My stomach hurt.

I said, "You *are* joking? Look, you know I absolutely need my own room!"

She looked like someone had just slapped her across the face. Well, too bad.

"I'm calling Dad," I said. "He'll get me a hotel room–like, with an *actual* bed."

She kicked that trundle thing so hard that it slid– *thwack!*— right back underneath. She swished past me, then stopped in the bedroom doorway. "Oh- *kay*. Well, Drey, it's nearly 10 o'clock in Dublin now, so your father and "Fee-Oooh-nah" are probably in or headed to bed.

"But by all means, Honey Bunny, you go ring your Dad."

Oh, God! Could someone please bring back my smiley, well-dressed and *civilized* mother?

I got Dad's voice mail. I texted him. Hey, Maybe he *was* already asleep. Or out somewhere.

Just like the rest of that flat, everything in Mam's kitchen was charity-shop old, including this little table and two stools.

Nothing matched and, of course, this entire kitchen was way smaller than the breakfast counter in Rutlinstown. I sat on a stool. Kept checking my phone.

She didn't look at me as she made scrambled eggs. Two slices of toast popped from a toaster. We ate in silence. After our dinner, she went to the fridge and took out a pint of Ben & Gerry's Chunky Monkey, my total favorite.

"Oh-huh, Mam. Yeah, that's reeee-al good," I said, sucking up a little now and mimicking Uncle Vinnie at my American wake party. I had to shout because another airplane was flying over.

Mam set down her ice-cream spoon and said, "Drey, please don't do that over here. It's rude to mimic people. How'd you like it if people started copying how *we* talk?"

What the hell did she mean, 'how we talk?' Check my phone again. *Nada.* Mam got up to plug in a kettle for tea. In a tight, brisk voice, she said she'd taken tomorrow afternoon off from work so we could visit my new school and get enrolled for September.

"But, like, aren't the schools closed for the summer?" I asked, through another spoonful of Chunky Monkey.

"Snow days," she said. "We had that big snow storm back in February, so they have to make up the days."

Whatever. She called this new school a "magnet school," so I pictured all of the American students glued together as they were drawn, by magnetic force, toward the school's front doors.

"It's a school that specializes in maths and science or STEM."

"What color's my uniform?" I asked. Still nothing from Dad.

"Oh, no. There's no uniform," she said. "It's actually a *public* school, but very hard to get into. I had them send me your report cards from Rutlinstown Academy."

Maths and science. These were my very favorite subjects. So score one for Mam here.

Mam had to be up for work and that hospital shuttle, so she went to bed really early. Turned out, that armchair in the living room was a recliner with a thing for your feet, and she brought me a duvet from her wardrobe and set an electric fan in the living room windowsill.

Yeah, it was hot, but I was so tired that I slept—until each night airplane woke me up again.

I got up to pee.

The bathroom had a slanted roof and one of those skylight windows, too. As I sat there, I thought the night sky and the stars looked like someone's framed painting just above my head.

I'm in America, I told myself. And my mother is there, just beyond this wall and her closed door. I thought of Freckle back there, in my empty bed at Granny's house. Or maybe she'd gone in to sleep with Gran tonight? On that toilet, I remembered something else Gran'd told me about those old American wake parties–like, the real ones from long ago. She said there were women who wailed and cried. Crying was, like, their official job. Did they get paid? I don't know. I doubt it. But wasn't there a word for it? Oh, yeah. *Keening.*

I was wiping myself off when the tears came—just a few first, but then, once they started, they wouldn't stop. I swayed back and forth on that toilet, crying. I was finally stopped and reaching for more toilet paper to blow my nose when more tears started. And if you asked me, I couldn't tell or say which round of tears was for which part of the shit show my life had become.

In Mom's bedroom, I could see the moon through the ceiling skylight. I didn't make a sound as I tiptoed across to climb into her bed. She reached across to tuck my arm around her until we both slept in America.

THE GRANNY FLAT

BEFORE WE'RE FINISHED EATING our Sunday dinner, my son-in-law Mark heads to the living room where he sits and checks his mobile–as if we've all been delaying him from something important. After dinner, I go in there to sit on the couch, while Lorcan, who's seven, rummages around on the hearthrug.

A "sectional couch." That's what Deirdre, my daughter, and Mark called it when that huge yoke arrived, shipped all the way from Boston to Dublin.

"We actually *have* couches in this country," I wanted to tell them, but since moving into my flat over their garage, I've been trying to keep my gob shut.

Some Sundays, Lorcan climbs and perches on the back of that couch and sits there, legs dangling, like a security barrier between his American father and his Irish granny.

Whenever I try to have a chat with the *ladín*, Deirdre always appears. And I've just given up offering to help her with the washing up or the tea tray, because all she'll say is, "Mammy, just sit and make yourself at home."

That's another thing I keep my gob shut about. Like, for all its grandeur, this Dublin estate house is a long way from my own home down in Cluainard, County Galway–and I'm not just talking about the miles or the motorway here. Since my husband Jack died, that house and land are sold and a new, strange man is driving his tractor across our fields.

Tonight, I hear the dishwasher clank shut. Mark pockets his phone. Then, here she is with our tea and dessert tray. Deirdre always takes the beige armchair. Some evenings, I imagine the three of us are on a television chat show where you sit where you're supposed to sit and say what you're supposed to say.

As usual, Mark talks to me through Lorcan, like, "Hey, Bud, did you ask your Grandma how her week went up there in her in-law?"

"'In-law' and 'Grandma' my arse," I'd really love to say to the *eegit*. Plus: "My name's *Margaret*, and in this country (which isn't your country, boyo), my flat is called 'a granny flat.'" Mark was a vice president at some computer place outside Boston, where our Deirdre met him. Now, after 10 years of marriage, he's transferred to the Dublin-Euro office, while Deirdre is director of marketing for a medical device company that manufactures (of all things) little yokes to put into your heart.

When Deirdre reaches for my empty dessert plate, that means that my weekly granny visit is over, and it's time to toddle back up those garage stairs.

On the way, the light on the outside kitchen door camera blinks at me. Some Sunday nights, I'm tempted to make a very rude sign at that bloody thing.

Upstairs, I switch on my telly and cross to close the front curtains. I'll never get used to all these lit-up houses out there, where strangers are eating *their* dinners or watching their Sunday-night telly. I feel like I'm standing in one of them observation towers at an airport. Speaking of airports, tonight, beyond the roofs and houses, two lights blink in the amber-lit sky—two airplanes waiting to land out at Dublin Airport.

A select area; a lovely estate.

Last year, when my son and daughter were coaxing me to sell up and move here, Deirdre had said this, hadn't she? And she'd said, 'We can't be worrying about you down there on your own, Mammy. And with work and everything, there's no way I can be driving across to mind you.'

And we want our little fella to know his granny.

Now, I wonder if she'd ever actually said that last part. Or did I just imagine it to make myself feel better?

See, when your husband of 47 years has just died and your two emigrant children divide up the money from their father's land, then set up video calls to plot and plan for your widowed life, you can't remember who said what. Or to whom. Or when.

Or if they said it at all.

Deirdre pays a woman to collect Lorcan from school. They pay a different woman to clean the house and yet another woman to come here to give him grinds and lessons in Irish because, 'we can't have him getting behind.' At seven years of age!

These days my mind often rambles, and I think a lot about how things can happen apart, but together. Like, that morning at the hospital in Galway, when something gurgled in Jack's chest and his head flopped back. I knew well he was gone, but instead of waiting for the chaplain, I went down the lift to the car park to stand inside the hospital railings. Double-decker city buses. Cars at the traffic light. Children on the footpath.

Everyone was off to work or school while my Jack's body was being wheeled out of the hospital ward.

Now, as those two planes wait to drop lower into the night sky, I close my living room curtains to go and sit in Jack's recliner armchair that takes up nearly half my living room.

Slap. Slap. Slap. Did I doze off during my Sunday-night film? *Slap. Slap. Slap.* It's on the other side of the wall, in Deirdre and Mark's bedroom. Gone now. So it was something on the telly. Or maybe I dreamed it.

I'm just tiptoeing across to my bedroom to turn on my electric blanket when there's a different noise. I go back to set my ear against the kitchen wall. Two cats are mewling. But they haven't a cat.

*

It's Monday afternoon, and here I am inside my little kitchen window, waiting for the after-school babysitter's car to come down the estate road. Right. Here she is, indicator blinking. In the front driveway she slams the driver's door shut to make a beeline toward the house, but where's Lorcan? Oh! Here he is, out of the car and heading toward the garden shed. In his maroon school blazer and gray slacks, the child looks like a miniature executive, not a *ladín* just in from school.

"Grandma?" says he, in that Yankie accent of his, when he spots me here on the driveway where he's kicking his football against the garage wall.

"Oooh! What a grand surprise, *Petín*! I was just going out for my walk. Tell me, had you a brilliant day at school?" He glances sideways toward the hedge, where his football has rolled. I scan his hands, his neck, his hairline. He goes over to get that football and comes back to say, "Mrs. Mullen said *our* reading group was the best!" The edgy look says he knows that this chat with Granny is naughty.

"Ooooooh!" I clap. "Brilliant! Do you like her, this Mrs. Mullen?"

He nods. Inside my head I hear those slapping sounds from last night. "Tell me, does she ever get vexed?"

"What does 'vexed' mean, Grandma?"

"It's when someone is cross. Like this.' I make a cartoon-y frown.

'Like my Mom sometimes, like, when she wants me to go up to bed?"

"When she's cross, does your Mam ever slap you? Even just a teeny slap?"

"No? My Mom says you should never, *ever* hit anybody. Like, ever."

"And what about Dad?" I'd put nothing past that fecker.

Lorcan sets his forefinger on his chin, as if puzzling over the answer to a very hard question. "Dad is just silly. But sometimes, he only reads me *one* story at night, even when I'm not tired yet.

And then, that makes *me* mad!"

"Lorcan!" The after-school sitter calls from the side kitchen door. "Come in and eat your snack and change now. Róisín your tutor'll be here in a minute." I pat my grandson's head, and I'm just turning back toward the garage door and the stairs up to my flat when he calls after me: "Grandma? You said you were going for a walk?"

*

This morning, Wednesday, I'm watching for the house cleaner, a nice-looking girl from someplace foreign by the looks. When she arrives, her car boot springs open and she comes around to lift out a plastic cleaning caddy. I pull on a raincoat and leave my slippers on to go down the garage stairs.

The gold crucifix on a chain around her neck tells me she's from a country where they still respect their elders. I shout louder than I should. "I am Margaret, Deirdre's Mammy."

"My name is Adriana," says she, as she sets that caddy full of squirty cleaning bottles on the driveway to reach back into her car boot for a hoover.

I picture Deirdre sitting in her office in that place where they make the heart gadgets. At this very moment, is she on her mobile gawking at me in my slippers and green raincoat?

Adriana crosses to the kitchen door. I act like I've something to ask her, so I follow her across. She dials in four numbers.

There's a buzzing sound. I stop, point down at my slippers, and make an 'oh-silly-me' face before heading back up my stairs. On my stairs I listen for Adriana to shut the door behind her before I go back down and sneak in there. Deirdre can't see me now. If Adriana catches me, I'll play the helpful granny just down here to rinse out their breakfast dishes.

The hoover noise is coming from the playroom. Brilliant. I

cross the kitchen to the front hall that's lined with framed photos of Lorcan as a baby and Deirdre and Mark on their wedding day.

That wedding was Jack's and my only trip to America. When those Boston airport doors slid open, it was like walking into a bloody fridge. I was ready for a cup of hot punch and bed, not a long drive to some lake in a place called New Hampshire.

The night before, Vinnie and Sonya, Vin's partner, had flown from London to Boston to stay in an airport hotel. When they came in the rental car to collect us, I was frozen stiff. Jack and I sat in, and the four of us drove on a motorway.

In the back seat, Jack slept and snored. I watched the giant yew trees. When I slept, I dreamed that I was flying with a big flock of geese, *flap-flap-flap,* all the way through the dark sky to Canada.

It's not right to snoop in your child's marital bedroom. I know that. But how else can I find out if that fecker is beating my daughter?

They have two built-ins, or "closets," as they call them. His side has a row of ironed shirts, white, blue and grey. There's another rail for his slacks and blazers, and a bottom shelf of shoes, runners and sandals.

In her built-in, I stoop to hang up a few of her blouses off the floor, but then catch myself. Can't leave any clues here.

The late-morning sun through their window reflects off something hanging from their padded headboard. It's a black, satin face mask, dotted with shiny sequins. Before I walk around to his side, I know exactly what I'll find in Mark's bedside locker.

A whip. Of course. Jesus! I'd read somewhere about this stuff of a man whipping a girl—or is it the other way around? Our Deirdre and Mark whip and whack loud enough to make each other mewl like bloody cats? Or is that exactly the point?

Honest to Jesus, I wouldn't put it past that fella to be showing off and taunting me through that bedroom wall.

I shove that whip into the waist of my slacks, where my green raincoat is just long enough to hide it from the house cleaner or if that door camera got switched back on.

Upstairs, my flat is silent as the grave. Until I lift my arm up high to lash that whip across the armchair. *Thwack, thwack.* As if you could or should beat the shite out of your husband for dying on you, for leaving you behind like this, a tenant in our daughter's house. *Thwack, thwack, thwack.*

Inside my head a little girl squeals, "No, Mammy. *Nooo!*" Our Deirdre. She's three years of age. The summer rain lashes against the window where, out there, our hay sits in long, dark stripes across our bottom fields. Vinnie, the baby, wails from his pram. In the living room, the Galway races are playing on our old telly.

Two minutes ago, Deirdre toddled in from the back kitchen, carrying her brother's dirty nappy from the soaking bucket.

She tittered as she ran toward me, that cloth nappy dragging and her brother's baby shit drip-dripping onto the floor.

Her blond hair is clipped back with a yellow slide in the shape of a duckling. When I belt her across the face, that slide tangles in her blond curls. *Slap again. And again.* Because I have to stop the rain and save our rotting hay.

Spare the rod and spoil the child. Back then, that's what people said.

It's four years later; a week after her seventh birthday. I've just come home from town after getting the messages and my hair done. I open the car door and she runs from the house (Mammy! Look!) waving a scissors. She's just chopped off her own and her brother's hair and now, the pair of them look like mongrel dogs.

Today, I take her father's belt to her legs. *Thwack.*

Thwack. Jack comes out to the yard to stand between her and me. *Jesus, Margaret. You'll kill the child.*

Over the years, the slaps got harder and longer. The legs.

The face. Back to the legs again, because they were easier to cover up by making her wear slacks to school.

Now, in my Dublin flat, I flail that living room armchair one more time, one final whipping and damning of the dead.

The graveyard silence is back. Maybe for the whole day. Maybe for every day to eternity. No. I'll escape from this place, this silent and 'select' housing estate.

I'll get the bus into the city center to find a shop that sells all those whips and kinky sex stuff. No. I'll find a Euro shop or a children's toy place to buy a little whip with pink feathers on the end, like in a pantomime or a circus. Oh, now. Won't this be great gas? Next Sunday evening, 'Grandma' will get up from the dinner table, *mar dhea* to "go to the toilet." After I've sneaked that pink child's whip into his bedside locker, Mister Mark will know what I know now.

I check my handbag for my glasses, my wallet with my free bus pass. I change the slippers for my walking shoes. This evening, when Deirdre doesn't hear me moving around up here, will she come up to check in on me?

The city bus is so crowded I have to sit upstairs next to a young pup with music twittering from those yokes stuck in his ears. I put on my spectacles to type, 'bargain shops, Dublin,' into my phone. OK, here's one called "EuroDeals."

We're off the motorway, and I'm still scrolling through that cheap Euro rubbish when the bus stops and waits at a traffic light. Through the bus window, I spot one of those big office buildings with glass walls in the front. Inside, four people stand, still as statues, at different spots on a moving stairs.

I'm back to that day, years ago now. In my mind's eye, our Deirdre is standing half-way up a set of moving airport stairs that keeps trundling up and up.

She'd finished at the Uni in Galway and started a job in a big office. Today, we had to drive her down to Shannon Airport for a higher-up job in the same company, only that office is in America. We've said our goodbyes and God bless. Jack has gone off to the airport car park. But here I am, people wheeling their suitcases around me as I watch our child, her back to me, as she stands up there.

I've something to tell her. I've a contrition to say, to make—

something for her to cradle and carry across the Atlantic. I race across the concourse to the foot of those stairs, where I tilt my head back to bellow her name: "Deir—"

—At that very second, a man makes an intercom announcement calling all passengers who are traveling to someplace.

She can't hear me.

That's why she doesn't turn around. As she steps off those stairs and walks out of sight, that's what I tell myself.

What We Remember

EVE IS COMING BACK from the Ladies when she spots a tall fellow pacing the hotel corridor outside the function room doors. A man bun, and the face is familiar. She must've seen him up at the wedding church and, in that getup, he's definitely on the groom's side. Hard to miss someone this rangy, tall and shabby and, Christ! What *is* that thing around his neck?

"Eve McManus; bride's side," she says, shouting over the racket through the function-room doors–that cacophony that the wedding DJ actually calls music. "I'm Cecelia's cousin; our late fathers were brothers."

He reaches to pluck an earbud from his right ear, then extends a handshake. "Terrence O'Leary."

Eve has always been taller than some of the men and most of the other women in her life–including her sister and her mother who are in there at their family guest table, also grousing over the music. But now, this tall fellow in his string tie (a medical alert button?) has to stoop to shake her hand. He says something else, but when Eve cups a hand around her ear to hear, he gestures his head toward the hotel foyer.

Yes, he's a first cousin of the groom. Earlier, he'd traveled up here from Cork to Kilkeera, County Clare on the bus–as in, the *public* bus.

"I really like your tie," Eve says, pointing at that thing around his neck.

"Thanks! They call it a bolo tie. It's a moonstone, and I got it as a present."

From a girlfriend or a partner? Oh, now. Why would she wonder or care about *that*?

A waitress in a crisp white blouse detours around them. She's carrying a black tray with a small teapot and a white cup upturned on its saucer. Decaffeinated tea. Water extra boiling. A drop of milk; no sugar.

Eve knows all this because, earlier, she and her sister Paula had to intervene between this waitress and Mam who screeches at foreigners–especially the ones who "refuse to learn or understand plain English." Now, Eve pictures her sister Paula and Paula's husband Jack in there, eyeing the door waiting for Eve to come back to resume her Mam duty. *Yeah, Paula.*

Well, I'm the one who had to collect her from her care home and drive her all the way down here and share a bloody hotel room with her.

Eve says, "Listen, Terrence, I think we're actually the only two non-partnered guests here. Fancy getting a quiet drink someplace?"

He nods, plucks out the second ear Bluetooth thing, and his right trouser pocket bulges when he stuffs it into his trousers pocket.

Outside, the town footpath is littered with Autumn leaves.

Half-way down the Main Street is a pub where two young men turn from their barstools to stare at them–a 58-year-old woman in her Arnott's navy-blue dress and high heels and matching clutch handbag, and this much younger man in his man bun–oh, and that string tie. Boho? Bolo?

"A gin and tonic," she tells the barman, as her phone beep-beeps from inside the clutch handbag she just set on the bar.

Jesus! Did this Terrence fellow have to slurp his Guinness like that, like, so loudly?

Terrence O' Leary says he's a musician and, five months ago, he moved back here from America–some town that doesn't ring a bell, but he says it's a suburb of Washington.

Her phone again. This time, she leans over on her barstool to reach into her handbag to switch it off.

"Since I moved back from the States I've been gigging here and there and I'm actually recording a CD—like, pop country and my own compositions. But, Jesus! You forget how bloody small this country is, and how it's all who-owes-who a favor and who'll scratch each other's arses."

As he talks, she watches them in the bar mirror, their faces framed together, like one of those old photo booths they used to have in train stations or tacky shops.

"What about yourself, Eve?" He asks. "How do you earn 'the ould crust of bread' as we say?"

"I'm a solicitor," she answers. "Mostly employment law. It was my late father's firm, just off Stephen's Green. Like, that's in Dublin."

He smirks. Of course, he'd know that already. Another loud slurp from his pint.

"Very nice. I'm actually going to be up there in Dublin myself in a few weeks—for the CD, and I've a promise of a few evening gigs in a place just off Liffey Street. Zanzibar. It's a pub and nightclub. D'ya know it?"

No. She hasn't been to a night club since college. Even then, she'd only gone once, with a few college mates, and hated all that sweat and dirt and noise.

An hour later, as they walk back up the footpath toward the wedding hotel, the two gins have made her wobbly. She brushes shoulders with a woman wheeling a baby buggy. The woman scowls, and Terrence catches Eve's elbow to steady her.

Her brother-in-law Jack is pacing in front of the hotel doors and smoking a cigar as he reads something on his phone. Look up here and see me, Jacko. I'm tipsy and walking with a tall young man. Worth the drive down here just to see the look on your smug face.

Jack pockets his phone. He frowns at Terrence, then calls across: "Ah, Eve, they're going totally mental in there. Your mother wants to be brought upstairs for her afternoon sleep, but you've the room key. Paula's been ringing and ringing you."

Next morning, Terence is downstairs at the hotel's breakfast buffet. No string tie today, just a faded denim shirt over rumpled combat trousers, and the man-bun is now a ponytail. He's scooping prunes into a white bowl.

"Ach, there you are!" He says, as if they'd planned this breakfast meeting.

Actually, she had.

Last night, once Eve got Mam settled into the second double bed in her room, she'd checked the Eircom bus schedule. The daily, south-bound bus from here to Cork leaves at 10:15. So here she is: up and dressed in a pink blouse tucked into black linen trousers.

A waiter crosses to their breakfast table inside the hotel's side window. "Tea or coffee there?"

"Coffee," they chorus, and, 10 minutes later, the waiter delivers a steaming cafetière for two.

"So what time'd you get out of there last night?" Terrence asks.

Oh, Christ. He slurps his coffee, too.

"Half eight. I'd had well enough by then."

Another slug. This time, the old woman at the next table looks over, frowning.

The waiter returns with a rack of toast. Terrence reaches for two slices, sets them on the white-cloth table. He makes two rasher sandwiches, then wraps them up in a white napkin.

"For the bus," he says, when he catches her staring. "I never waste free food."

She asks, "Where will you stay when you come to work in Dublin?"

"Found a few things online. Dublin—actually, this whole country--is gone ridiculous now. Ah, sure, once you let the capitalists and the multinationals take over, the ordinary, working person always gets screwed."

"Well, give us a shout when you're up in the big smoke."

From her leather handbag she hands him her business card: Eve J. McManus & Co., Solicitors. Earlier, back in her room, she'd written her personal mobile number on the back.

A fortnight later, they're sitting in a café in the Powerscourt Center where he's propped his black guitar case on the chair next to him, like a third lunch guest.

On her walk down here from her office, she'd taken off her trouser suit jacket and untucked her blouse to look better, jauntier, maybe even younger.

Terrence says that, as well as that music gig at Zanzibar, he's found a small recording studio and a place to stay at a city-center hostel.

A hostel? Eve pictures snoring illegal immigrants and criminal drug addicts.

"I have a spare room." She says. "I'm out in Rutlinstown, but we're very near the DART or rapid transit. And it has a very good bed." Oh, no. Did the bed mention give the wrong impression?

He swallows a forkful of his quinoa salad, then waggles his head left and right, as if he's dithering between two viable options.

"I don't want to imp–"

"—Look, I wouldn't offer the room if it weren't available–at least 'till you find something... well, other than a hostel."

Three hours later, she leaves work early to collect him from that recording studio that, from her car, looks like an abandoned shed. From there, they drive south across the city and out to her two-story *maisonette* in Windsor Terrace.

The McManuses are from Dun Laoghaire, not Rutlinstown.

But after Daddy died, she and Paula and Mam had sold the family house, then divided up the furniture and tidbits. Eve bought her luxury maisonette and, as the older, spinster daughter, she installed their mother in the front, downstairs room with its own *en-suite* bathroom.

Last year, Mam had her hip replaced. Three days after her mother's hospital discharge, Eve came home from work to find that Mam had sacked both the visiting nurse and the physical therapy man. Next day, over a very long and tense phone call, Eve persuaded her sister Paula that they absolutely had to move their mother into a care home with rehabilitation services, and she'd found one already, though it was way out west of the city, in Lucan.

"Only if we can all agree that this is just a *temporary* measure," Paula said, in that tight voice that sounded much more legal than Eve's. On that call, Eve imagined her yummy-Mummy, housewife sister mentally subtracting the care-home fees from the money in their family trust.

In Rutlinstown, Eve disarms the security alarm to lead Terrence O'Leary down the short hallway. She winces as the guitar case whacks the door jam and he sets it on the polished-wood floor of Mam's room.

A killing silence. Is she supposed to stay? Leave? Play the hotel porter and give a little bow and wish Mr. O'Leary a comfortable stay?

"OK making up the bed yourself?" She asks. "There are sheets and a duvet on the top shelf of the wardrobe."

Upstairs in her own room, she changes out of her gray suit into yoga pants and a cotton sweater.

Later, as she drains their dinner pasta, she thinks she hears his footsteps creaking across her dining room. Nothing. She sets the colander aside to tiptoe down to Mam's room where she's just about to knock when she hears a whispery voice. He's in there on his phone.

Back in the kitchen, she texts him that his dinner's ready. No response. She sets two places, but eats alone at the breakfast counter, where she keeps the radio off to hear him.

Later, on her way up to bed, she listens at his door again.

Snores now—though not as loud as Daddy's used to be.

Next morning, as she sets her briefcase on the car's passenger seat, she sees that his window blind is pulled all the way down.

That evening, the window blind is half-way up. The security alarm hasn't been set and, inside, except for her cafetière and one cereal bowl drying on the dishrack, there's no sign of her house guest.

"Your Mammy moved back home again?" Samantha, their office legal assistant, asks next day, when she walks into Eve's office to find the boss-woman checking her mobile–again.

The rest of that week, on client calls or at meetings, Eve checks and checks her phone. At home, a new feeling creeps into her house—actually, her whole life.

It reminds her of their childhood summer holidays down in Connemara, County Galway—where the McManus family spent every July in a rented holiday house that stood in a horse-shoe of five lookalike houses, all of them overlooking Galway Bay.

Back then, the minute they passed Palmerstown, the younger Eve always tried to forecast which exact holiday house they'd get. Next, she imagined up the new summer friends she'd meet this year—including boys. Just like in those novels she read in bed, she and her new friends would host secret beach picnics and they'd chase each other into the sea or spend the mornings sailing beneath a blue sky.

Three hours later, when they finally arrived and Daddy turned the key, the holiday home always smelled musty. Still, she raced through each room to find the treat, the big surprise that she'd told herself would be here and that, just like the summer friends, turned out to be more fiction than fact.

Now, she's actually glad that Terrence doesn't know or can't be bothered to set the security. The damn thing takes too long in the evenings when, just like her younger self down in Galway, she uses the home-commute time to predict and imagine exactly where she'll find him. Sitting on the living room couch, playing guitar? Or out in the tiny back garden drinking coffee?

Or reading? Does he like books? She never asked.

But except for the cafetière and that cereal bowl on the dishrack, there's no sign—and no note or text. Honestly, if it weren't for the drawn window blind every morning, she'd wonder if he'd moved out.

On Thursday, she plunks her after-work wine on the kitchen counter and walks across the dining room and down the corridor to push in that bedroom door.

No guitar against the wall. His bed is unmade. On the mahogany dressing table sits a black contraption with a red, blinking light. A music recording gadget? Some sort of surveillance device? You never knew these days. Just in case, Eve assumes a frantic look, and, if asked later, she'll say that something got stuck in the kitchen sink, and she needed after-hour plumbing help.

Later that Thursday night, at twenty past two in the morning, she wakes to the sound of a rattly car exhaust. She gets up to raise her bedroom window blind. Out there—across the estate's central lawn, Windsor Terrace is shut up and silent.

Wait! Three houses up, and almost out of her sideways view, is a small, black hatchback with the engine running. She's turning back toward her bed when the passenger-side door opens. Terrence. He's stooping to call something back in at the driver, then shuts the door to stride up the footpath, guitar in hand, down toward her house.

Back in bed, she hears that car rattling around Windsor Terrace's central green. The residents' association will complain.

I'll knock on his door and talk to him about it. Tomorrow.

Friday evening, she's coming home from work when Paula's

name flashes on the car Bluetooth. No. She won't answer, because a Friday call from her sister means only one thing.

Paula's two kids have a Saturday recital or rugby practice. So tomorrow, Eve's sister can't drive to the care home to collect Mam to take her for the usual Saturday sleepover and for the family's Sunday lunch. After that lunch, it's Eve's job to take their mother back out to Lucan and the care home.

Eve is just turning into her driveway when here's the inevitable follow-on text: "Can U collect Mam and bring her there 2moro, then out here on Sunday, then drop her back Sunday night as usual? Need to know ASAP. XX."

"ASAP, my foot!" Eve says out loud as she bangs her front door shut behind her. After the usual listen at Terrence's door, she thumps upstairs to change. The guilt creeps in. Maybe she *should* go and get Mam to have her stay here tomorrow night?

She could ask Terrence to book a night in that hostel. While Mam's here, she could break the news to her: Remember that man we saw down at Cecelia's wedding? The tall one in the shabby clothes? Well, Mam, he's living here now—like, as my ...

tenant? No. As my *friend*.

Mam would be appalled. No. It's too soon for a bombshell like that. So she'll wait. And it's better to tell Paula first. Mam actually listens to Paula.

Back downstairs, Eve finally texts Paula back: "Sorry missed call. Can't collect Mam 2moro. Friends coming over. I have plans."

Paula answers: "Plans???"

Eve texts back a smiley face.

She's pouring her after-work wine when here's another text:

"No worries. Jack says he can go out and get Mam." This text has no kiss or heart emoji.

The 'have plans' thing wasn't entirely a fib. Now, half-way down her bottle of Cabernet, she realizes that, all week, she'd been counting down to tomorrow, Saturday, when she and Terrence will actually be here together—at least until his evening performance at Zanzibar. So she'll make them a nice late brekkie or brunch, and they'll sit and talk—just like housemates do. He likes rashers. So she'll get some of those good rashers from Norton's, the artisan grocery and butcher's down on Rutlinstown's Main Street.

Next morning, she's coming back in from the back garden, clutching the last of the Autumn asters for the table centerpiece, when she hears music. He's setting the cafetière next to the electric kettle. When he spots her, he fumbles in his jeans pocket.

Music stopped. He frowns at the asters, then looks back through the kitchen door at the dining room table that's set for two with Mam's wedding china.

"Eve! You're ... ah ... here!"

"I'm just making myself an omelet. You'll join me? I hope you like goat cheese, and I have rashers from our butcher down on Main Street. Sausages, too. All locally sourced!"

Why does he look so edgy? Trapped?

"Jeez. That's awful decent of you, Eve, but I ah ... have to go into town early, then I'll just stay in there for my gig. You know how the bloody buses are. Especially on a Saturday."

Her voice comes squeaky-high. "Oh! Yes! No problem! I actually have two friends coming over. We take turns hosting a Saturday brunch, and I thought you might like to join us. But no ... ah ... no problem! I'll ... *We'll* leave you a plate in the fridge. Like, for later?"

"Grand." The voice is conciliatory. Is she hearing pity? He reaches into the overhead cupboard for the coffee mugs. "Join me for a quick cuppa?"

"Yeah. Go on," she says, as she sets the asters on the breakfast counter.

"Your week went ok, yeah?" He asks, over his shoulder. He pulls open the cutlery drawer for spoons. All so easy, familiar to him.

"My week went fine! Yeah. Actually, it was a bit busier than usual. Is ... is your room OK? You're comfortable in there?"

"Oh, Eve. Will you stop? It's a thousand times better than anywhere I've kipped up for the past five years. Rents in America are absolutely mental! All gentrification and multi-millionaire property investors and pushing out the working man."

The electric kettle boils. Clicks off. He fills the cafetiere and adds, "Oh, and the working *woman*. My bad there; yeah, my bad, Eve."

Beware the legal client who uses your name over and over. Daddy always said that. But they were different times, and, except for his wife's china on her dining table now, Daddy is dead and gone.

Terrence hands her a mug of coffee. He opens the fridge door, holds up the milk carton. "I take it black myself, but I remember from that morning after the wedding that you take a drop of milk in it, yeah?"

He remembers how she likes her coffee. No, this man, who's actually a family relation, is just a kind, creative person who's doing her a big, big favor by staying in her spare room.

She nods toward the second kitchen stool, but he stays standing there in front of the kitchen sink, looking down at her.

Slurp. Slurp. Oh, yes. How could she have forgotten the slurping?

As well as his musician friend in that rattly car waking the neighbors, she's going to have to bring this up with him, too.

For his own good.

He glances at the microwave clock and slugs the last of his coffee. "Sorry, gotta go. Have an appointment at the recording studio—like, to talk over the contract and all that."

"I'll drop you into town," she says.

"But what about your friends?"

"I ... I can text them. They're always late anyway."

"No, no. I'm grand. Honestly. Listen, you girls enjoy yourselves, and don't do anything I wouldn't do, ha, ha!"

Across the kitchen counter, she watches him eyeing that

brunch table again. And, by that look on his face, her story about fictitious friends has helped him decide something.

After the front door bangs shut, her phone dings. It's Paula, texting to ask if she, Eve, could please bring a side dish for their Sunday lunch tomorrow.

"If it's not too much trouble," her passive aggressive sister types. As if, for the past ten-plus years, Eve hasn't *always* brought the side dishes for their family Sunday lunch. Fine.

She'll use the veggies she'd chopped up for this morning's omelet to make a ratatouille, which none of them—especially Mam—will eat.

That Saturday night, Eve wakes to the rattly car again. This time, she can't be bothered getting up, so she clicks on her Kindle audiobook, stuffs in her earbuds to get back to sleep.

Her mattress is tipping. She must have been dreaming she was on a boat. No. Terrence is sitting down there, on the end of her bed. Or is it Terrence? Yes. The tall, naked torso is backlit by the landing light. He's swaying. The room is silent. He keeps swaying. Back and forth, a human pendulum.

The mattress tips again. OK, he's leaving. Shouldn't she ask if he needs something? No, he's flopping onto his hands and knees and crawling, like a dog, with that bolo tie dangling from his neck. He edges back her duvet and eases into her bed.

After their intercourse, he does what all of her old boyfriends used to do: He lies there on his back; the hands clasped under his head. Is she supposed to pat his shoulder and say something here? Like, "Good job! A-plus!"

Mam spends most of their Sunday lunch complaining about the care home's food and saggy mattress and all the cheeky, ungrateful foreigners who work there.

Jack—good old Jack—has spooned some of Eve's hastily made ratatouille onto his plate–right between the slices of roast pork and roast potatoes. Between bites, Jack winks across at Eve and flashes that auto-smile of his, like an airport customer service person waiting out someone's mad rant.

Meanwhile, Paula gives Eve the raised-eyebrow—the look that says it's time to move their mother back to Windsor Terrace, where it would be easy and cheap to install a few grab bars in that downstairs bathroom.

Today, Eve doesn't care about Mam's grousing and Paula's looks and how she and Jack always speak to her through their kids: *Tell Auntie Paula about the science fair at school.*

As she chews on a slice of roast pork, she imagines lobbing her big, *big* news over Paula's Autumnal-themed table centerpiece: *No. Mam can't move back in with me. Not now that I'm having wild sex with my housemate. Not housemate. Partner?* Yes. Partner. That's who Terrence O'Leary is now.

The clocks changed, and the dark winter evenings came early and damp. Now, every day and hour of Eve's working week register or count according to how much time is left until Saturday night when Terrence comes upstairs to her bed again.

Week mornings, his blind is still pulled down. Evenings, he's out of the house until the early hours. On Thursday nights, she hears his musician pal or colleague in that rattly car. Saturday nights, he's there on the end of her bed again, swaying back and forth.

Some evenings, in the silence of that house, she's tempted to go snooping in his room again. Looking for what? Evidence of him looking for a flat share in town? No. He won't move out of here. Not now. Plus: She's not going to take her chances with that contraption blinking from the dressing table.

My partner. Oh, how she loves dropping that word into work conversations, relishing the look on her colleagues' faces. *My partner did this. My partner said that.* My *young* partner, she'd love to add, but now, that *would* be tacky, right?

"Awwwww," Amanda at work said, that first time Eve had said it. Amanda's little blond head was tilted to the side, as if she'd just found an abandoned kitten in a rubbish bin. "Well, I'm delighted for you, Eve; Really, I am. It's like they say: It's never too late for anyone."

Eve will wait until she and Terrence have taken the next step, crossed the next hurdle in their relationship, before she tells the family.

Now, weeknights, she pours her evening wine and plots how to make this happen, to force her and Terrence's affair forward and make it overflow her upstairs bedroom to all the other parts of their shared house. A kiss by the kitchen sink? A snog (or more) on the living room couch? A walk, hand in hand, around the estate lawn where the trees are already strung with white Christmas lights?

Monday evening, December 3, she finds a yellow envelope among the pile of junk mail on her hall floor. Addressed to Terrence. The sender has written, "Birthday boy" on the envelope's back flap. Eve slides it under his bedroom door.

Tomorrow, she decides, upstairs, as she steps out of her work trousers. It's his birthday. So it's time for their next step.

Next morning, she writes a sticky note and ties it with a ribbon to the handle of the cafetière: "A little birdie tells me it's someone's birthday soon! Dinner and pressies here at 6, E. xx.

All day, she checks and checks. No text, but she pictures him with headphones on as he sits in some glassy booth in that recording studio. So out of phone range. Of course. Yeah.

She leaves work straight after lunch to stop at Norton's on Main Street to buy two servings of potato gratin, two small steaks and a bottle of very good champagne.

At home, it's just past three o'clock, but the window blinds are pulled all the way up. Good. Yes! Awake and here and ready to celebrate. *With me!*

His room door is ajar. But no Terrance. In the kitchen, that ribboned note is gone from the cafetière. She sets the food and champagne on the kitchen counter and rushes to his room.

The dressing table is covered with dust. That blinking gadget is gone. On the mattress sits a pillowcase stuffed with his sheets.

Except for that string tie thing dangling from the hanging rail, the wardrobe is empty.

With its black-painted interior and faux candles, Zanzibar looks and feels funereal. The barman says, "No, sorry. Yeah, Terrence plays the bar here–but only Thursday and Saturday nights–like, before our big shows out back."

Eve asks, "So he's playing tomorrow? Can you please double check?"

The barman takes a phone from his pocket. "Yep. He's on the schedule for tomorrow!"

Jeez, why has she always been such a worrier? Terrence has moved out because he's just found himself a flat share; someplace closer to the recording studio and this dive. Once he's fully unpacked in his new place, he'll ring. He'll visit, come to stay with her on Saturday nights. Or he's left her a note back at the house that, earlier, she was too flustered to notice.

She's in her car, indicator on as she waits for a break in the Saturday-night traffic. A tall, gangly girl stands staring across the footpath at her. Twirls her hand, signaling for Eve to open the car window. Over there, across the footpath and outside Zanzibar's door, three youngsters are standing, obviously waiting for this girl, their friend, in her black, puffy coat.

Well, Eve McManus wasn't born yesterday. She knows that muggers often use a decoy to build trust, to make you let your guard down so they can rob you blind.

Eve releases the car clutch to move forward. But instead of scampering away, the girl follows, raises a halting hand. Eve puts the car in neutral and dials 999. Ready to just hit that emergency number if needed.

She opens her car window.

"Yeah, Hiya. Evelyn, isn't it? I'm Lizzie, Terry's girlfriend. I'm just heading out with my friends here, but I saw you so I just wanted to say a quick 'hello'!"

"Sorry, you have the wrong pers–"

"—No, you're Terry's Auntie Evelyn, right? I recognized your lovely car. Like, from outside your gaf?"

Across the footpath, a young man calls, "Lizzie, are ya comin' or not?"

"Terry's a considerate fella. He never let me drop him off directly outside, 'cos he said you were such a light sleeper—like, from your cancer chemo treatments."

The boy at the pub door shakes his head, then opens Zanzibar's door, while this Lizzie stays babbling through Eve's open car window. "... I'll tell you, he'd better not be that slobby in my place. No way, *José*. Anyways, did we forget something? And you came to drop it off for him? Awww. That's really lovely, so it is, especially when you're still sick and everything."

It's January 5th, and this week, Eve and Mam have been watching a Netflix series about an English woman who gives up her busy London life and job to move to Tasmania. There, she's bought and is rebuilding an old shack. Predictably, a dishy Tasmanian lives right next door. It's not a bad series, but every night, Mam's red walking aid blocks the full view of their television screen.

Tomorrow, Eve and Mam will drive out to Paula's, where they'll eat their usual luncheon and the last of the Christmas pudding. January 6th is "Women's Christmas," which, this year, feels like someone's appalling joke.

Two weeks ago, just before the January fees were due at the care home, Paula and Eve had driven out to Lucan to pack up Mam's clothes and tidbits. Paula consented to splurge on a new, orthopedic bed for the downstairs room. As the two furniture delivery men carted the old bed up the corridor and out through the maisonette's front door, Eve remembered all her dead relatives' funerals—including Daddy's —and how the pall-bearers carried the coffin from the church at Dun Laoghaire to the hearse and, later, the family burial plot.

Eve spent the week before Christmas going to a city-center

hotel for lunchtime interviews with candidates from an elder-care agency. Finally, the day before Christmas, she hired a woman from County Roscommon who spoke perfect–though *culchie*–English. Tomorrow when she leaves for work, Eve must remember not to set the security alarm so that woman can come in here to start her daily elder-care visits.

By now, Eve and Mam have run out of things to say. So thank God for the telly where the Netflix Londoner and her dishy Tasmanian have finally collapsed, half-naked, onto a backyard hammock.

Mam's nodded off for the raunchy part. Good. Eve eases out of her armchair to shunt the red walking aide a few inches to the left, for a full view of that tanned, half-naked man.

As that Tasmanian garden hammock swings and rocks, Eve wraps her arms around her own torso. In her armchair, she rocks herself, back and forth. It's a commemoration of all those Saturday nights when a tall man came to sit on the end of her bed.

A Loveless Match

IT'S the small things you hate a man for. She should tell this to all those young women who phone in the radio or write to the magazines with their tales of woe about wandering husbands.

She certainly wouldn't mind Tom wandering—not that anyone in their right minds would have him. No, it's the small things, like his smelly socks under the range, false teeth on the back kitchen window, and, this morning, a jam jar of his own, human dung in the fridge.

The dung must be to bring to the doctor in town. For medical tests. Like, what else would he want it for?

Whatever his plan, she opens the fridge and moves that jar aside to reach the butcher's parcel of stewing beef. Today is Tuesday, when they always have beef stew for the dinner.

At the table under the window, she chops off the fat and slices the beef into smaller bits, then crosses to the kitchen range to drop these beef chunks into the melted butter.

For years it's been this red casserole, this wooden spoon, this cream-and-black kitchen range. Sometimes, she thinks that, even if she lost her eyesight, she could still find her way around and still get the dinner and make bread in this kitchen.

Later, a few hours from now, he'll come tattering in from the fields, still smelling of tractor diesel and musty hay. He'll push his food around on the plate, pretending to eat. Then, a quick look at the kitchen clock, and off with him like the hammers of hell. He can do nothing in time. The man will be late for his own bloody funeral.

Back at the window, she starts peeling carrots—long, thin slices slithering into a tin basin set in the sink. She knows he'll say nothing to her, as if a man keeps samples of his own dung in the fridge every day of the week, and as if she needs doctors or tests to tell her anything.

She pushes up the window. It's too hot on this August day for the range lit in this big kitchen with its green painted walls and the blue and white floor tiles.

He laid those tiles when she first came here. No cheap linoleum, she'd declared as a young bride; hadn't she enough of that in her father's house? Back then, Tom would've done anything to this house just to please her, to smooth the edges of her bustling, blunt ways. But everyone around here knew that theirs was no love match.

Love matches. That's all they talk about nowadays—on the radio, on the telly, as if the whole of Ireland were a dog in heat.

On her shopping days in the town she sees them—these youngsters with their phones and their school skirts up to their back sides; their faces lifted boldly to the sky, as if all the world were waiting for them. Some of them titter as she walks past--an old, head scarfed woman lugging bags of messages to an old, jiggety car with a trailer hitch on the back. Tell those young girls you married for a house and 42 acres of land and to avoid going back to work in America, and they'd laugh their tinkling laughs and tell you to go on with your oul'

yarns; sure that kind of thing only happens in black-and-white films.

In the films nowadays, America is always loud—a cop shouting, a gun detonating, a woman screeching or banging her fork against a restaurant table.

It's been nearly 50 years now, but in her memory, America is always ghostly quiet. Or was it just Doctor Lodge and his wife's Boston house? The only sound she can conjure or remember is the ticking clock on the living room mantel. Elsewhere–in the kitchen, on the landings, in her maid's room on the third floor–

someone has turned off the volume. She can't even conjure the traffic or street sounds out there, at the end of Doctor Lodge's stone steps. And, though she can see that dance band on stage at the Irish dance hall over in Roxbury, she can't hear the chat or tunes. Not anymore.

The Lodges had a huge kitchen sink. She remembers that, and she can picture herself standing there, in a white apron over her blouse and pleated skirt, chopping and slicing raw vegeta-bles. Doctor Lodge liked summer squash. Roasted. No salt. Oh, and maple syrup. Janey, she'd forgotten about that until now, today. *Maple syrup*. Funny how these kinds of things resurrect in your memory at strange times and for no reason—as if they're here now, in her own kitchen.

She'd married Tommy Kearney to escape that doctor's red-brick house with its sideways view of the trees in the Boston Gardens. In winter, from her third-floor maid's room, she could see the stone statue of George Washington on his horse.

That summer of 1960, eight years after she'd emigrated, she hadn't wanted to come back here to County Mayo. But Dr. and Mrs. Lodge were getting a new roof, so they were leaving to spend the summer up at their place on the North Shore—that big, seaside estate he'd inherited from his father and grandfa-ther. Waverly, that town was called, though it was a village not a town, with a tiny train station and roadside stone walls and all those grand estates perched above the sea.

She'd actually been there once, to help with some lunches and dinner parties for his brothers and a few cousins who'd traveled from other states and places. Once the main course was served, she remembers sitting out on their big, wooden veranda over the sea.

That summer of 1960, the Lodges had hired a local girl to

cook and clean at that North Shore place. So after eight years away from home, she'd decided to fly back on an Aer Lingus flight that, in those days, took way longer than seven hours.

Jim, her older brother, had inherited their father's land. Her sisters were all married to men with their own farms of land. At her childhood house, Jim's wife, Bridie, resented this summer visitor, this returned yank in what was now Bridie's own home and kitchen.

One night, at a marquee dance, Tom Kearney asked her onto the floor. Shuffling around that dance floor, she wondered if people thought that this man in a Sunday suit and tie was actually her father or uncle. By night's end, he asked if she'd go dancing again.

Just before it was time to go back to Boston and her job, he proposed. As he asked, she pictured her Boston maid's room with its big bed and the winter snow on the windowsill.

Already, after just one summer back home, that word— *home* —had become a big huge lie. Or it was just a child's storybook word with no real place to match it. So she married Tom and moved into this house.

Now, she reaches into the bread box to tear off a chunk of white bread and jam it between her teeth, like a horse with its bit. Then, she slices into the huge onion that, two days ago, Tom brought in from the garden.

Long ago, her mother had taught her to hold a bit of bread between your teeth so that onions don't make you cry.

After the wedding breakfast, he'd driven her to Salthill, Galway, where he'd booked a bed and breakfast for three days.

That bed and breakfast was on a side street, just off the promenade. In the evenings, he treated her to buns and tea in a café.

And the nights, she remembers those too, the grunting and fumbling, and her relief when it was all over, when they drove back here to this house and the fields where every perch, every stone in every wall on this land would become as familiar to her as her own hair.

During that first cold winter, when he was up half the night with lambs dropping, he asked where was the sense in them both missing sleep? He'd moved into the small, back bedroom.

When he never returned to their own bedroom at the front of the house, nothing got said between them.

Every night now she hears him shuffling down the corridor and then in the toilet, heaving, heaving, as if his thinning body would turn itself inside out altogether and flush itself down the hole.

Chop-chop. The bit of bread is doing its trick today. No onion tears. *Keep chopping*. Make him eat his usual dinner before he has to leave for the doctor in town.

Some days, the dark things flit around the edges of her mind, like a wasp in the window. She sees and remembers, even when she's busy, even when he isn't here: his hollowing eyes, the way his neck no longer fills his Sunday shirt, the shadows of pain that cross his face when he thinks she isn't watching.

A month ago, she caught him down in the far hay shed, asleep, his arms cradling his body like those pictures of unborn babies. She left him there. Later, when the radio played from its shelf as they had their evening tea, she asked him nothing. She owed him that discretion. God knows she had and kept her own secrets.

Back at the range, she dumps the tin bowl of chopped carrots, onions and parsnips into the red casserole. She adds water from the kettle, sprinkles pepper and salt and moves it all to the oven.

*

When they returned from that honeymoon, he'd surprised her with a stone garden bench that he'd commissioned from a local stone mason. For warm summer days, he'd said. She could sit and rest herself out here, just like those bed and breakfast guests they'd seen in Galway.

Today, her bench is mottled with yellow lichen and moss.

Everything in this garden needs to be cut down, tidied. For years, there were too many other things besides sitting outside or fussing with flowers: summer hay, winter fodder, cattle driven through dark, wet fields and loaded onto trailers for early morning fairs and cattle marts.

A lone calf bellows in the bottom fields. Tom is down there, somewhere, shuffling between his sheds and stone walls. Killing time.

She blows her nose on her cotton apron, and then holds on to the wet patch, twisting the damp cotton into a tight, hard lump.

How would they end their days, the two of them? He wouldn't hear of hospitals; she knew that. And soon, he'd grow frailer, weaker, sleeping like a baby all day. And she would have to clean him, turn him, empty the bucket in his room. There'd be doctor's visits--the door closed softly on the patient as the young face sitting across the kitchen table from her talked diagnoses and advice for the almost widowed. But what prescrip-tions has he for a wife who's terrified, not by death, but by the strange, body intimacy that sickness always brings?

Up in the village, the 12 o'clock Angelus bell rings. Long ago, she'd stopped praying. But she crosses herself now. Should she go in and ready something for his trip to town? A clean shirt?

His good Sunday shoes?

She stays put; her strong body on the stone bench. She'll keep things the same: cows milked, the dog fed, cattle foddered, bread in the oven and dinners on the range. And today, when he reaches into the fridge for that jar of dung, she'll turn her back and pretend not to see.

This is what she could tell those skittery young girls in the town and on the telly. This is how our sensible marriages live and survive.

They find their own way, like a three-legged dog who keeps walking.

ATTRIBUTIONS

"TRESPASSERS" was previously published in *The Larcom Review*, Vol. 3, 2001 and in *Lost and Found: An Anthology of Teachers' Writing*, 2003.

"A Fine Lady Guest" was published as "A Most Regrettable Occurrence" in *Litro UK*, 2013.

"The Man on the Train" was published in *Women Writers. Women's Books. An audio version was published in The Drum: A Literary Magazine for Your Ears.*

"Snow" was previously published in *Books Ireland*, September 2000 and by Pixel Hall Press, 2014.

"A Loveless Match" was previously published in *The Literary Review*, Vol. 44 and by Flume Press, 2010.

"House Devil" was published as "Detonating" in *Spire*, 2006.

ALSO BY ÁINE GREANEY

Fiction

The Big House

Dance Lessons

Nonfiction

Green Card and Other Essays

Writer with a Day Job:

Inspiration & Exercises to Help You Craft a Writing Life Alongside Your Career

About the Author

Born and raised in rural Ireland, Áine Greaney now lives and writes in coastal Massachusetts. In addition to her published books, her short works have appeared in Creative Nonfiction, Another Chicago Magazine, The Boston Globe Magazine, The New York Times, Books Ireland, WBUR/NPR and other publications. Her work has been nominated for a Pushcart Prize and cited in Best American Essays. She designs and leads creative and wellness writing workshops.

About the Press

Sea Crow Press is an award-winning woman-run independent book publisher based on Cape Cod in Massachusetts committed to amplifying voices that might otherwise go unheard. We publish creative nonfiction, literary fiction, and poetry. Our books celebrate our connection to each other and to the natural world with a focus on positive change and great storytelling.

9 781961 864207